The Map of Me

The Map of Me

Tami Lewis Brown

FARRAR STRAUS GIROUX
New York

Text copyright © 2011 by Tami Lewis Brown
Distributed in Canada by D&M Publishers, Inc.
Printed in July 2011 in the United States of America
by RR Donnelley & Sons Company, Harrisonburg, Virginia
Designed by Roberta Pressel
First edition, 2011
1   3   5   7   9   10   8   6   4   2

mackids.com

Library of Congress Cataloging-in-Publication Data
Brown, Tami Lewis.
    The Map of Me / Tami Lewis Brown. — 1st ed.
        p.   cm
    Summary: Twelve-year-old Margie finds her sister, Peep, intolerable since the
youngster skipped from third grade to sixth, but when their mother leaves home,
Margie packs Peep into their father's car and starts driving across Kentucky to find her.
    ISBN: 978-0-374-35655-2
    [1. Sisters—Fiction.   2. Family problems—Fiction.   3. Self-actualization
(Psychology)—Fiction.   4. Automobile travel—Fiction.   5. Kentucky—Fiction.]
I. Title.

PZ7.B81794Map 2011
[Fic]—dc22
                                                                                    2010029261

For Jill

The
Map
of Me

1

My pencil scraped a skinny gray line across the newsprint, then a square, then a triangle on top. A house. A teeny-tiny house for teeny-tiny little—

"That's ugly," Peep said. But her voice was the ugly thing, as high-pitched as a kindergartner's, even though she'd had her ninth birthday last October.

Still, I threw my pencil down. I was no good at drawing, especially drawing a Map of Me.

"Homework!" Momma said, like one word was threat enough. Okay, it was. I picked up my pencil and started again. And Momma flipped through a catalog of teeny-tiny-house plans, keeping watch, one eye on me, the other out the kitchen window. She'd have a two-minute warning before Daddy walked through the door. Plenty of time for a smear of Coral Sunset lipstick and a splash of eau de cologne, which was the mannerly way to say toilet water. And the good and proper way to say "Welcome home!" to Daddy.

Momma was not the only one watching me. The biggest chicken collection in the state of Kentucky winked and grinned from every surface. Poultry potholders and pitchers, hen's-nest holders and rooster racks, all staring down at me.

Plus there was Peep. "My map is finished," she said. "I turned it in yesterday."

Peep did everything before it was due. She'd kept quiet through kindergarten, first grade, and second, too, pretending to be normal. Then last fall she blabbed, spilling smart right and left, learning stuff before any teacher mentioned it, before she saw it in a book, probably before scientists, and professors, and mathematicians invented it. She sat in third grade for three weeks, until her teacher begged for mercy. They tried her in fourth (week and a half), then fifth (less than an hour). Finally they shoved her up to Miss Primrose's sixth grade.

My grade.

My class.

No fair.

Momma was oh-so-proud. Daddy said they'd have put her in high school but she was too short for the desks.

I hoped she'd grow soon.

Or something worse.

My tennis shoe thumped against the rail of the hard kitchen chair as I scribbled some more. A bird on top of that triangle roof, a little rooster weather vane, like the one Momma had just ordered.

I hated homework.

I double-hated the Map of Me.

During quiet time after lunch, Miss Primrose read to us from a book called *The Hobbit*. Lots of kids were happy because teachers didn't read out loud to sixth graders, not usually. It meant we wouldn't have silent-at-your-desk work. But I didn't listen to Miss Primrose's boring words. I just heard the rumble rumble of her voice, the buzz of the fluorescent lights, and Jimmy McDonald's steady breathing in the row behind me. And a million different thoughts chitchattering inside my head.

Then Miss Primrose turned the whole story time against us, using that book to justify her Map of Me assignment. Because J. R. R. Tolkien, that author, he imagined Hobbit-land and wrote the book about it. Then he let his son draw a map for the front. Not just a map of Hobbit-land, it was a map of Mr. Tolkien's insides, his brain, and his heart, too. He let his kid stick his nose into every private place. And print it down on paper.

That was not going to happen to me.

Not for everyone to see.

I shoved my pencil into the page and added another bird. And when I pushed my pencil to draw his triangle beak, the paper ripped in a row of mini-pleats.

"That's really ugly now," Peep said.

Shut up! I wanted to say back, but "shut up" was a cuss-word in our house, and I was on probation. Instead, I wound my arm around my page, to make it private.

"Hush, girls," Momma said. "Your daddy's home."

The front door jangled. Daddy-size footsteps clomped through the living room, and quick! Momma rolled her catalog into a little bat and slapped it behind her hen-and-chicks cookie jar.

Peep grabbed the placemats.

I rubbed my eraser across my messed-up chicken and made a bigger mess.

Then Daddy was in the doorframe, right in front of us. His white work shirt was still starchy-crisp and his tie was still knotted tight. The very picture of Mr. Super Salesman. Daddy had a talent for tires, that's what they said. There wasn't a rim or a hubcap he couldn't tick off, manufacturer's suggested retail price and everything. Daddy knew his tires all right. And he knew me. At least he thought he did.

"Hi, Daddy," I said, sitting up good and straight.

"Get back to work, Margie," he said.

He pecked Momma on the cheek as she wiped invisible spots from the counter with a sponge. "Sell a lot of tires today?" she asked.

He grunted and leaned toward the cookie jar, and Momma practically threw her body between him and those chickens. "You'll ruin your dinner," she said.

"Just a little snack." Then Daddy took a step, his eyebrows twitching like a pair of fighting caterpillars. "What is this?" he asked, pulling the booklet from behind that cookie jar. "'Backyard Chicken Coops for Fun and Profit'?"

Peep gripped a placemat. Momma put down her sponge. I stopped erasing. All of a sudden the kitchen smelled like singed feathers.

"Live chickens?" A vein strutted up and down Daddy's neck, and Momma's shiny black eyes darted left, then right.

"Live poultry is where I draw the line," Daddy said.

He'd drawn the line lots of times. No more roosters in the dining room, because their staring put him off his feed. No more chickens on the refrigerator door, because you couldn't pull out a bottle of pop without the whole flock dropping all over your feet. "My collections make our house a home," Momma had said. "More like a barn," said Daddy. But Momma'd waited and Daddy's lines had

7

faded, until they evaporated out of sight. Now our dining room had a brand-new Randy Rooster wallpaper border to show for it. Daddy didn't look up when he ate.

But this was different.

"No live poultry in the backyard, Helen," he said, so loud the chickens rattled on their racks.

Wipe.

"I'm just talking reasonable," he said.

Swish.

Then Daddy stomped out of the kitchen and out the front door.

Gone.

2

Days went by, till it was practically Valentine's. But I wasn't feeling so lovey-dovey, walking home from school, wind skittering between my jacket buttons, mean and frisky. I was hot inside. Overheated.

Peep skipped beside me, cool, cool, too cool. She jingled like one of Santa's elves, pockets stuffed with dollars changed to dimes, two bucks for every A. Sixty dimes rattled with every step, like she was one big A+.

"Why didn't you turn in your map? Now it's too late," she said, cheerful, like me getting an F made her the luckiest sister in the world. Sometimes I wanted to grab that golden ponytail and snatch her bald-headed.

Momma claimed she called her baby Peep because she looked like Little Bo Peep from our Mother Goose book— golden curls, rosebud lips. Daddy said she never made a peep when they brought her home from the hospital. But now she wouldn't hush.

I knew the truth. With that yellow blond outside, Peep was a candy chick in an Easter basket. Fake sugar sweet, with an alien brain whipped out of weird chemicals and marshmallow cream unknown to the natural world. She made me sick to my stomach.

"I got an A on my map," she said, as if I hadn't heard, twelve times at least, since Miss Primrose handed back the papers. "You're just lucky you didn't break Jimmy McDonald's ankle in that *unfortunate square dance accident*," she added, like she thought my small situation in the gym wasn't any accident at all.

This morning Miss Primrose had announced our class Valentine's party would be Appalachian Ethnic Dancing, which was prissy-pants schoolteacher talk for a square dance.

Most of the sixth grade moaned, but Jimmy, eyes so green he looked part Martian, he didn't seem to mind.

After lunch we marched to the gym for practice. We took off our shoes so we wouldn't mark the gym floor. I curled my toes up so nobody could see the almost-holes in my socks.

Miss Primrose put on the music, and when the man

sang out "Take your partner," she picked Peep, even though she wasn't a boy. Peep was her little pet.

Jimmy McDonald scooted in front of me.

Me?

Oh.

Jimmy McDonald had never noticed I was alive. Not until today.

But I had noticed him.

My mouth went dry and I hoped I wouldn't throw up, and all through "Slide, slide, and dance just so" his fingers tingled my wrist. Not just my wrist. All the way up my arm and across my shoulders.

Jimmy's eyes flashed, as bright green as a traffic light. Go. Go. Go. But I couldn't look. I stared at his socks. White, with a stripe across the toe almost as red as my face. No holes.

Breathe. Jump. Breathe. Jump. Breathe.

When the man sang "Take another partner and you Jump Jim Joe!" Ellie Moore pushed. Jimmy gripped. I squirmed. Then she shoved, but he held, so I yanked.

And he flew . . .

    like a cyclone,

      across the floor,

        into a heap.

Jimmy limped and Ellie cried.

Peep put the blame on me. "I bet he'll never pick *you* again," she said, jingling across the Martins' driveway. "And I bet his ankle is broke."

"Then you bet wrong," I said. "Step on a crack, break your momma's back." And Peep almost fell on her face, stumbling at the join between curb and sidewalk.

I tried to run ahead, but she caught up. "You should be the one worried about Momma," she said. "Momma'll break *you* when we get home."

No.

Momma would be quiet. Momma would be sweet. Momma wouldn't even notice.

"Good thing for you Daddy's working late," she said.

Good thing for me.

"Peep, Peep, what a creep," I chanted under my breath, and she smacked me, knocking my binder to the ground, spilling math worksheets across the sidewalk.

C−

Needs Improvement.

$2x < y$

Two x's are less than a y.

$M < P$

Margie is less than Peep.

Correct.

Peep shoved the papers practically up my nose and rattled on down Pine Street, me trailing past the Madisons' yard of weeds ("town menaces" according to Daddy), by Mrs. Bell's prize-winning lilac ("just right for a widow woman"), past the Rogerses' crooked mailbox ("not one scrap of pride"). Their windows were lit up like the Kountry Kollectible Koops Momma kept on the dining room buffet. $14.99 each! Kollect the Entire Barnyard!

All up and down our street, families got ready for dinner. "You wash your hands, baby?" "Who's saying grace?" They ate meatloaf and mashed potatoes in kitchens that smelled like cinnamon toast. They smiled and told funny stories. After dinner they played Monopoly or Go Fish. All together.

The kids were cute. The daddies were happy. The mommas had fun.

They didn't have evil genius sisters.

Finally, I stomped into our yard, across Daddy's carpet of green needles, my big feet crunching a size-eight path of destruction.

Our porch light wasn't on.
There was no car in the driveway.

13

* * *

Momma's car must have been parked somewhere else for the afternoon. Oil change. An eighteen-point valve inspection. No problem.

"She's probably at school," Peep said. "Meeting with Miss Primrose. About you."

Breath slipped from my mouth in cloudy puffs. Cumulus. Stratus. Cirrus. Nimbus. All the formations I missed on the last science quiz.

Momma's latest crafty creation welcomed us from a nail on the front door: her Valentine's wreath, a million pink feathers hot-glued and stapled into a fluffy "I Love You." I tried the door, but it wouldn't open, so I pulled at the string twined around my neck and took the house key, warm from my own heart. Momma said this key was for just in case, but just in case was not supposed to happen.

I twisted my key into the lock and swung the door open, and Peep rushed past, running through the living room, headed for the kitchen.

I leaned against the doorjamb, cold, cold, cold against my cheek, closed my eyes, and whispered to myself

a secret—

no, a wish—

no, a prayer:

"Just once let me be as good as Peep."

3

"Margie, come in here." Peep's voice echoed through the dark house.

I stumbled past the living room, busting my shin on the coffee table. Olde English Rose air freshener stung my nostrils. Momma was a big one for scent.

Peep stood in the middle of the kitchen, hens and chicks watching and waiting. "Momma's gone," she said.

"No." Momma was here. Okay, lots of times she was good as gone, rearranging her chicks into cute little scenes, dreaming of one last figurine to complete her set. But Momma was always home, in body if not in soul. She cooked. Peep did her homework. I pretended to. After dinner, Momma wiped the kitchen clean while Daddy yelled at the ball game or the news on TV, like the team and the president needed his advice.

Peep pointed at the magnets on the refrigerator. A fat

momma hen plumped her nest, a rhinestone rooster pounded a tiny plastic piano. Magnets covered every inch of the freezer and most of the fridge.

These were fine collectibles. The mail order catalog promised they would rise in value. Momma's fancy magnets didn't work for a living, holding dumb family pictures or boring school notices—

Until now. A ratty scrap of paper dangled behind a cannibal chick, waving a sign for Frank's Barbecue.

"What's that?" I asked.

Peep peered at the paper. "It says 'I HAVE TO GO.'"

Something tightened inside me, wrapping around my guts, twisting like wet shoestrings tied in double knots.

"Momma signed it." Peep snatched the sheet from the refrigerator, waving the page toward my face. Her voice was squeaky, more babified than ever. "She wrote her whole name: Helen Marie Tempest."

"Give that here," I said.

Peep twisted her arm behind her back, but I was stronger. I pulled until I had the paper clenched in my fist. It just ripped a little.

I HAVE TO GO.

Solid as words carved on a tombstone.

This was crazy. Momma did not "go."

The second hand tiptoed around her Three French Hens wall clock. Quiet. Not a tick.

"She's gone for a walk," I said, even though the only place Momma walked was down the grocery aisle.

Peep blinked. Her eyes said, *This is all your fault,* but her mouth kept still. It might have been better to have Daddy home stomping around than to be surrounded by all this silence.

I turned to the stove. A pan of mushroom soup sat on the back burner, little brown floaters bobbing to the surface. Momma was not exactly a super-great cook. She went more for presentation. I stirred the soup, around and around and around, until it swirled into a foamy gray whirlpool. "Maybe she's out buying crackers," I said. That explained it. I was the Queen of Reasonable Explanations.

Peep pulled the cabinet door open and slammed a box of saltines next to the sink. "We have plenty of crackers," she said, loud, way loud. Maybe quiet was better after all.

"She's just . . ." I started to say. Just what?

Peep began shoving stuff across the counter, like she expected to find Momma hiding behind her hen-and-chicks cookie jar. "If she's here, where are her canisters?" She pointed to the corner by the fridge, home base for the Little Red Hen flour, sugar, and whatnot jars. $29.95 per month, with Clucky Lucky FREE to the first hundred callers. Momma had collected those jars, one at a time, over four years. She'd just needed one more, the Henny Penny Coin Canister. Then everything would be complete. But now Momma's cupboard was bare. They'd flown the coop, every one.

I had no reasonable explanation for that.

Peep trotted upstairs as I opened the refrigerator, matter of fact, like all I wanted was a snack. Like it was normal for a lady to go for a stroll with her canisters, leaving her family with nothing but an I HAVE TO GO. And a pot of rubber soup. I stared at the refrigerator shelves. Burnt sugar pudding, sour cream ambrosia. All in tidy rows, wrapped up tight. Crushed pineapple, chipped beef, diced ham, neat, in alphabetical order, practically.

Before I could pull out a plate, Peep lunged back into the room, cheeks pink, breathing hard, like she'd run the Field Day 50-yard dash. "Her suitcase is gone."

Momma wouldn't haul out her Samsonite on a whim. You did not take luggage and an armload of canisters for a trip to the grocery store, or to a parent-teacher conference.

Peep was right. Momma was gone.

I slammed the refrigerator door and chicken magnets hailed down. Beaks and claws clattered around my feet, spraying across the linoleum. Tears welled in my eyes, sharp as vinegar, but I couldn't let Peep see. I bent to the floor, pretending to herd the chicks back into the fold. When Momma got home from wherever she'd wandered off to, she'd be fit to be tied if her poultry had a chipped feather or a broken wing. I gathered a handful of magnets and placed them on the counter, careful.

In a trance, I pulled bowls from the cabinet and moved to the stove. "Have some mushroom soup," I said. That sounded responsible. Soup calmed people down. They ate it in movies, after disasters. Movie stars with blankets wrapped around their shoulders ladled soup into their mouths. Then the hero came to the rescue before the whole universe exploded.

We needed that hero here, right now.

4

A beige skin had formed across the top of the pan. I tore it open and spilled soup into the bowls, dribbling goo over the sides. Mushroom soup wasn't that great of a goodbye meal, but it was Daddy's favorite.

I hated mushroom soup.

We did not have war heroes or movie heroes in Ithaca, Kentucky. All we had was Daddy. Flat-Tire Fixer. Ithaca High Volunteer of the Year.

Maybe Daddy could save the day.

Last fall, I found a copperhead in the backyard, by the pile of brush. I poked it with a hickory stick and it struck, fangs bared, body arched and writhing While Peep stood there screaming "Snake!"

Daddy ran out of the house, fast as lightning. He snatched me up, nearly wrenching my arm from the joint, and he grabbed Peep, too. Carrying us high, almost over his head. Then he plunked us down on the picnic table. Safe. There should have been music in the background. Trumpets maybe.

Then he went back with the garden hoe and chopped the snake into itsy-bitsy slices. In a flash! That snake never stood a chance against Daddy. He wasn't even breathing hard.

Peep shoved the cracker box and the soup bowls across the counter, mad, like they were the ones who'd done something wrong.

"Daddy's fast," I said, like I was talking about a relay race. "He'll catch Momma."

"Call him," Peep said. "Now."

My hand twitched as I lifted the receiver and punched in the numbers for Daddy's work. Each glowing button squawked like a banty rooster.

"World of Tires," Miss Jeannie Fainshaw answered, sappy sweet. I could practically see her through the phone wire, tapping her nails against the customer service counter, breathing through her nose, nostrils flared.

"This is Margie. I need to talk to my daddy."

"Marjorie Ann." She went from honey to battery acid in one second flat, soon as she heard it was me. "Your daddy is striking a deal on a new set of radials. He can't be pestered by the likes of you."

The phone clicked and the dial tone buzzed dead. No chance for me to beg that this was a really-true-this-time major emergency.

"What did he say?" whimpered Peep.

Too busy. Can't be pestered. Nothing. I bet Pretty Princess Peep wouldn't have received that response. If it had been Peep, Miss Jeannie would have been "Oh, sweetie! When we gonna see you down to the store?" Daddy would have hopped to the phone, radials or no radials.

I smiled so big my lips ached.

"Daddy said come on," I said. "He said run!"

5

We bolted out the back door, kitchen lights blazing, soup left glopping on the stove. I ran first and Peep followed, pulling on her jacket, one arm, then the other.

When we got to World of Tires, Daddy's face would be blustery—his two little girls invading his place of business, reporting to God and his manager and every living soul how his wife had left him. In front of the other sales associates, he'd act like we were playing a big joke, the kind with a hidden camera, the ones people sent in to television. Hilarious Videos of American Families.

He'd let out one of those rough chuckles, like a goat swallowing a ball of string. Ed and Joe would laugh, too, pretending me and Peep were a couple of pranksters. Ha. Miss Jeannie would nibble her lipstick with a smirk, and tap, tap, tap the counter with her witch claws. Then Daddy would drag me and Peep to the parking lot, pinching the top of my arm a little too tight.

But he'd still save the day. He'd still be our hero.

Me and Peep ran around the house, out to the sidewalk. "Take the shortcut!" I yelled.

Mr. Johnson said he'd build a house in the lot at the end of the road when he got the money together, but for now it was still a field, overgrown and wild. We both pulled up short at the edge of the grass.

"There are rattlesnakes in those weeds," Peep said.

"That's just what the high school kids say."

Peep's feet grew roots through the concrete sidewalk.

"The snakes are asleep," I said.

"You mean hibernating," Peep said, her being the family expert on snake habits, along with everything else. She took an almost-step, hand twitching at her side, like she expected me to grab it. Like she thought we should cross through together.

She could forget that.

"Snakes can't catch me," I said, taking off through the grass. Briars tugged at my pants, and I didn't look down, just in case. And I didn't wait for Peep.

Somehow she made it through, jingling through those weeds. Maybe snakes are afraid of A+ grade money. On the other side we ran-walked, past the Watsons' house, yard bursting with bicycles and wagons and every kind of ball. Then the Stephenses', with Christmas lights still dangling from the garage eaves, then the Bells' and the Peterses' and a whole bunch of others.

We rounded the corner, and Ithaca unfolded in all its glory. Lazy Forks Luncheonette, Jip's Drugs, the Whatnot Shop. At the end of the block, the World of Tires sign glowed, each neon letter buzzing with white-hot brightness.

I ran through the parking lot and Peep grabbed my shoulder. "Don't you go in there and make him ashamed of us," she said. But Miss Bossy didn't need to tell me how to act. I wouldn't rush into Daddy's store, screaming "Momma left us" or "We've got to drag her home, now." Daddy was an important member of the World of Tires team. I wouldn't embarrass him.

Not too much.

But by the time we wiggled up to the big plate-glass window even Peep realized there was no need to yank my arm or shush me up. Neither one of us was moving a muscle.

Miss Jeannie was up front behind her little desk, orange hair stacked on top of her head like a roll of brand-new pennies. She was not the kind of widow-lady who grew lilac bushes in her front yard. She tilted her chin toward the plate-glass window and her eyes narrowed, like she saw me and Peep out there, like she defied us to walk through the door.

The air hadn't gotten any colder but Peep shivered, pressing up against me.

Daddy was to the left, customers huddled three deep around him. He was World of Tires' Super Sales Associate, commander of the sales floor, grinning like the Big Bad Wolf, tapping the tires with the tips of his fingers, explaining something serious, like the traction ratio of Weatherwhackers versus All-New Ultrabelt 360s. Another five minutes and he'd have every one of those people convinced he knew more about steel-belted radials than anybody in the whole wide world. The Commonwealth of Kentucky, at least.

Another five minutes and Momma would be who knows where.

How about an extended warranty to go with those hubcaps? And a World of Tires credit card, too?

Miss Jeannie grinned, and the customers smiled, and Daddy laughed out loud.

Not his goat laugh.

Daddy laughed big, and deep, and jolly as Santa Claus, so loud it vibrated through the window. He didn't laugh like that at our house. Not even on Christmas Eve.

Ho Ho Ho.

Then Daddy tipped his chin to the glass, like he saw us. Saw me. He looked straight at me. His eyes got squinty and he shook his head. No. No. No. He waved his hand. Get on along. Shoo! Then he turned away and kept on talking.

This hero was too busy for the likes of us.

6

Me and Peep backed through the parking lot, but before we even made it to Jip's Drugs a big blop of wet fell on my shoulder, then another on my head, and quick as you could say Jack Sprat it was raining. Really raining, fast and hard, like in summer, but cold. Icy February sleet ran down my neck and soaked through my shirt.

Daddy's car twinkled under the World of Tires parking lot security light. Not every vehicle was as lucky as Daddy's Ford. He polished it to a heavenly glow every Sunday afternoon, after he was done with Good Grace Church of the Redemption and his plate of fried chicken. When the other daddies stretched out on the couch, digesting, our daddy had a job to do. World of Tires customers were 57 percent more likely to buy a set of radials from a man who appreciated his own automobile.

"Come here," I said, tugging Peep toward Daddy's car.

"I'm going home," she said, but she didn't pull away.

"We'll go as soon as the rain stops." I opened the driver's door and Peep climbed in and I yanked the door shut behind us. "It can't last long, coming down like this." Grownups said things like that about rain.

I leaned back, wet and cold all the way through, all the way down to my everlasting soul. The kind of cold that hot chocolate or sweaters or fireplaces couldn't heat. Daddy's jacket was wadded on the seat next to me, soft and faded from a hundred cycles in the washing machine, a thousand days on Daddy's back. I slipped it on.

The jacket smelled of clove aftershave and the bacon-cheddar biscuits Daddy slipped in his pocket mornings he worked opening the store. A whiff of ink from an old ballpoint that leaked in the pocket, its oily stink left along with the mark. Old Gold Filters he'd borrowed off Al and smoked behind the World of Tires. What Momma didn't know wouldn't hurt her.

Soft and sad had worked into the jacket's old plaid lining, leftovers from a thousand days on Daddy's back. Time and space were grooved into the corduroy. I pulled the front closed, tighter than the zipper, but I still didn't feel warm.

Peep blew foggy clouds onto her window and squeaked out shapes with her finger. She drew formulas: x's and y's and $\div$'s and π's. Weird stuff, way beyond my wavelength. Another universe. Andromeda. Or wherever Peep brains came from.

Daddy would not like his windows smeared up like that, even if it was math symbols. Even if they were drawn by his Pretty Little Princess.

"Give me Momma's note," I said.

"I'm busy."

I grabbed Peep's jacket and stuffed my hand in her pocket.

"Stop it!"

"I want to see—"

Peep shoved me away with her left hand, pulling the note from her other pocket with her right, slapping it on the car seat just out of my reach. "There!" she said.

Fine.

I picked the note up and flattened the wrinkles against the steering wheel hub.

I HAVE TO GO.

No. She did not. Momma did not have to go. Anywhere. What she had to do was stay with us. With me.

I HAVE TO GO.

Why?

A grand idea blossomed inside my brain, full and round as a pink Bazooka bubble. A reason. One that would make sense. Snap.

"What if Momma's one of those people you read about in the grocery store checkout papers?" I said.

Peep stopped smearing her window. "Huh?"

"What if Momma's a woman of mystery, with three or four secret families hid all over the country?"

Slowly, Peep turned toward me.

"What if she has a little girl, and a little boy, too? And they live in Tuscaloosa. The little boy plays Little League and the little girl has curly hair."

"You're such a liar," Peep said. "You make up stories about everything. You don't know the truth from a lie."

Fine. It was a lie. A big fat lie. But telling it, I'd almost believed it myself.

Our momma wouldn't just leave. There had to be a reason.

"I didn't want to scare you," I said. "But I think Momma was kidnapped."

Peep's eyes went as round as a pair of Super Tread-blasters.

"Momma's the identical twin of the queen of a

faraway land. Not real twins, they just look exactly alike, down to that birthmark under her left ear."

"I have a birthmark like that, too." Peep tossed her ponytail over her shoulder.

"Yeah," I said, narrowing my eyes, staring at her neck, like I was taking measurements. "That queen is bad sick and they can't let her subjects find out. For security reasons. You know how that is."

Peep nodded like she was the worldwide expert on royal security.

"Spies kidnapped Momma to be their fake queen, until the real one gets better. Or forever if . . . Well, I shouldn't say . . ."

Peep sat still for a minute.

The rain hammered on.

"That's stupid. Spy kidnappers don't let you pack a suitcase before they carry you off," she finally said, folding her arms across her chest.

"'Stupid' is a cussword," I reminded her, and she kicked me for real this time.

I watched the rain run down the windshield.

"Why did she leave?" Peep whispered, so quiet it was barely more than a breath.

I was afraid of the true answer. So finally I just said, "I don't know."

7

My finger traced each letter, the start to the stop of the "I," up and down, to the around and around of the "O," on and on, forever.

I HAVE TO GO.

Why? Where?

The paper was torn and wrinkled, nothing but a scrap from some old advertisement. This was not how somebody wrote they were leaving. When somebody said goodbye they did not put it on a piece of trash. They wrote it on a sheet of fancy paper, the kind Momma used for notes to old women, saying she was so very sorry their cousin dropped dead at the reunion, or her Christmas letters full of exclamation marks, telling how this had been an exciting (!) and successful (!) year for the Tempest family.

I turned the scrap over to read the shiny print on the back. A porcelain chick blinked out at me, feathers glittering. "The deluxe limited edition Henny Penny Coin Canister," the caption said. The precious baby of Momma's flock. The only thing Momma lacked. A cute speech bubble curled from Henny's beak. "Y'all come to the Second Annual Rooster Romp! February 14, International Poultry Hall of Fame," she chirped. It seemed like Momma's missing chick had passed down a commandment: "Come!"

Clear as a cut-crystal barnyard bell, I knew where Momma went.

She had not run away from us, not exactly. She was running *to* something—to the Romp and her missing chick.

So what about us chicks left behind?

Peep yawned way too loud and I stretched my foot to tap the pedals.

Gas.

Brake.

Brights.

I had the longest legs in the whole sixth grade. Boy or girl. Longest arms, too. Gorilla arms. We measured in class, all lined up against the wall. At least nobody asked shoe sizes. Lining up by shoe size would be worse than tallest first. Why didn't they just use alphabetical order?

"When can we go?" Peep asked.

"Soon as the rain lets up." It was streaming now, pelting the roof like BBs.

But Peep couldn't be quiet and accept it.

"No. It's not going to stop," said Peep. "This is precipitation in advance of a cold front." She sounded like the Channel 3 weather girl, except Peep actually knew what she was talking about. "It's traveling on the winter gulf stream. This rain could last for days."

"Oh," I said. Why couldn't some gulf stream pick me up and carry me away . . . fly me to Momma, romping with those roosters at the International Poultry Hall of Fame.

Now Peep was on a tear. "The system picks up moisture over the Gulf of Mexico, then . . ."

I turned to my window and squeaked out pictures of my own. Long squiggly lines. Roads through my Map of Me. This was how it really looked, tangles of roads that stretched to nowhere.

"Once a thermal mass begins to build . . ."

I tuned her out. You couldn't give her too much encouragement. One little word and she'd set off on a lecture, like I'd begged, *Please tell me every single thing you know about the weather, goldfish life cycles, or how they make jelly beans.* She'd tell it all, by the hour, half made up, probably, her squeaky voice buzzing like a fat spring fly beating itself against a windowpane. *Zzzzzz—zzzzzzzz—zzzzzzzzzz!* Peep was relentless.

The air was stuffy with Peep's cotton candy breath and my wet tennis shoes, and finally, a heavy blanket of quiet. So quiet an idea started building inside my brain. Momma and the Rooster Romp and . . . "Jimmy McDonald can drive a car," I said.

"Right. Like I believe that."

"It's true. I heard him tell it."

"Margie and Jimmy sitting in a tree, k-i-s-s-i-n-g."

"Shut up," I said. "I don't even like him." More like Jimmy didn't like me. Besides, I had something more important on my mind. "Jimmy's daddy took him out on Route 11 and tossed him the keys."

"No way," Peep said. "Jimmy's not old enough to drive."

"You're not old enough for sixth grade," I reminded her. That shut her up.

Jimmy told it all last Wednesday, on the way in from recess. I hid behind the classroom door so he couldn't see me listening. He described how he turned the key in the ignition and how he shoved his foot on the gas. All the boys stared like he was the Second Coming. Then he held his hand out straight, twisting it left and right, like he was driving a race car, showing how he'd cut the corners and banked the turns. The boys oohed and aahed. I swallowed hard and watched.

"I drove over ninety miles an hour, flying. Probably hit a hundred, but the speedometer's broke," he said.

I twisted the Ford's steering wheel and touched my toe to the gas. How could he have gone that fast?

Jimmy's daddy was proud as a peacock, sitting in that passenger seat. Jimmy said so.

My daddy was, what? Cursing me behind the World of Tires' plate-glass windows? No. He hadn't noticed a thing.

The rain poured and Peep sighed, and I tossed Momma's note back onto the car seat, my hand brushing the Arctic Velvette upholstery. Daddy's Ford was some vehicle all right, blessed with eternal new-car smell. No ice cream or pop had ever dripped in this car. Not even once.

I knew how to drive, too. When I was little. When I was practically an only child. Before Peep talked. Before I was the dumb one.

I was four, and Daddy put me in the car. He sat me on his lap because I was his special girl. He placed my hands on the wheel and said, "Take her, Margie. She's yours." I steered, bending his old Ford around corners, across intersections. Daddy pressed the pedals because my legs wouldn't reach.

I drove then.

And I'd drive now.

Daddy was too busy. So it was me and Peep and this Ford off to the rescue.

8

I bent over and slid my finger across the carpet, hunting for Daddy's spare key. No sticky candy wrappers or chewed-up gum on the floor of Daddy's car. Nothing to embarrass.

"What are you doing?" Peep asked.

"We're going to the International Poultry Hall of Fame," I said. "To get Momma."

Peep stared at me like I'd grown two heads.

"They have rare chicken collectibles. It says so, right on the back of Momma's note."

"We don't need more chickens," Peep said. "And Daddy doesn't get off work until eight."

My fingers found the key under the edge of the floor mat—sharp, cold, the key to my salvation.

"You don't know how to drive," Peep said, smug, the

way she was when I didn't know my spelling words, or couldn't solve my math homework.

"You've just never seen me," I said.

"What about a driver's license?" she said, like that won the argument.

Leave it to the creep to bring up paperwork. "Driver's licenses don't mean a thing to anyone, except police. I'll drive careful. Flench, where they have that chicken museum, isn't far. It's barely down the road."

She shook her head.

"This is an emergency," I said. "That's an exception to the driver's license law."

"No exception I've ever heard of."

So Peep was a baby lawyer, too, not just a mini-doctor and a junior rocket scientist.

"You can't take Daddy's car," Peep said. "It's stealing."

That was the dumbest thing I'd ever heard. Borrowing something from your very own daddy was not stealing. No way.

Peep reached for her door.

If she went to Daddy, she'd ruin everything.

She'd tell him I got a zero on the Map of Me.

That I tried to steal his car.

That I broke Jimmy's ankle.

And that Momma left us. For chickens.

He'd explode.

Or he and Miss Jeannie and Ed and all the customers would laugh out loud.

Peep lunged for the door but I was too quick. I hit the lock button and she was stuck.

But she would see. It would be like when Miss Primrose assigned me to work with Arlie Simms. He only brushed his teeth once a week, but he knew how to work the eyedropper for science experiments, one teensy drop at a time.

I knew how to drive and I knew how to find Momma. Peep would appreciate me, once she understood.

"This is kidnapping," she shrieked. "Open the door."

No way. Who'd ever heard of kidnapping your own sister? And who'd want to kidnap Peep?

I turned the shiny silver key over in my fingers and slipped it into the ignition.

Click.

Perfect.

Meant to be.

Peep wrapped the seat belt round and round her hand till her knuckles went skeleton white.

But I didn't care.

I was in the driver's seat now.

9

I twisted the key in the ignition but the engine sputtered, then died. *Clunk Clunk.*

Daddy never had trouble getting the Ford to go, even on cold mornings. Maybe it was broken, or jinxed. Or loyal, like an old beagle who only did tricks for his master. Daddy's Faithful Ford.

Clink cachunk.

"See, you don't know how to drive. Just like you don't know how to do quadratic equations."

So what, and she was wrong. Wrong about the driving anyway, not about that math. I didn't even know what a quadratic equation was. I didn't want to know.

"It needs gas," I said. That was driver talk. My language. I stretched my foot deep, pumped the gas pedal, and turned the key, all at once. Come on, Ford. Run for me.

"You're going to kill us," Peep said.

Wrong. I was saving us. I was a hero in the making.

I twisted the key and the Ford sputtered awake, engine snarling mad.

"See," I said.

"We aren't moving."

Creep.

"What about lights?" she asked, quiet, like she wasn't sure she wanted to help.

Lights. Lights. Yes. The windshield was wet and fogged up, and I couldn't see across the parking lot, much less down to the road. I wiped a clear patch of glass with my knuckle, and searched the fake wood dash, scattered with buttons and dials. Cruise control. What was that? Climate monitor, no. Headlights, yes. I pulled the knob, and watery beams glowed from the Ford's grille. My hands curled around the steering wheel, natural. I was ready to roll.

"Windshield wipers," Peep said.

I found the switch and pushed it all the way, and the windshield wipers set off flying.

Whap Whack Whap Whack.

The sound of Momma's staple gun, pinning those bird feathers onto her Valentine's wreath.

Whap Whack Whap Whack.

The sound of Miss Primrose's chalk, attacking the board.

Whap Whack Whap Whack.

The sound of my heart, pounding to escape.

"Let's go," I said, like me and Peep were really in this together.

She wrapped another loop of the seat belt around her hand and didn't say a word.

Fine. A quiet Peep was a good Peep.

A little window behind the steering wheel showed the gears. "D. That means drive," I said, sitting up as straight and proud as a high school driver's ed teacher, showing Peep what was what.

"D is for dead," she answered.

Big-brained baby.

I pulled the gear lever down. Why did grownups make such a fuss, pretending driving was a big deal? Setting rules that you had to be sixteen to push a little pedal and putt-putt-putt down a road? Driving was no harder than riding a bike. It was easier. With a car you didn't have to pedal. I tapped the gas and the Ford quaked like a wild animal—an old mean one, stirred from hibernation. A rattlesnake, probably. Or a bear.

Then we lunged forward, straight for Miss Jeannie's Toyota.

"Brake!" Peep yelled.

My foot danced across the floor. Where was it? Next to the gas? Was I supposed to push the brake with my right foot, same as the gas? Was I supposed to drive two-footed?

"Stop!" Peep braced her hands against the dash and closed her eyes.

She was right. I was going to kill us before we even left the parking lot.

Then my foot found a pedal.

I stomped hard and hoped it was the right one.

The Ford shuddered to a stop, rear end dropping.

Bounce, bounce.

Plenty far from Miss Jeannie's dumb car. Feet, practically. Okay, inches. Still, not a scratch.

Peep was shaking all over, voice, body, everything. "You did that on purpose," she said. "You're a safe driver? A driving genius?" Peep yapped like a pink Chihuahua. "You have no idea what you're doing. You're an ignoramus."

If she thought vocabulary words would make me quit, she was wrong—100 percent incorrect. Maybe I needed a teeny bit of practice, but that almost near mistake proved something. I knew how to react in an emergency. "I'm a perfectly fine driver," I said.

"You're a perfect lunatic. I'm going home," Peep said, tugging the door handle with all her might.

"Can't you see I'm trying to drive?" I said, just like Daddy. I pulled the gear lever again, R this time. R was reverse, behind, backwards. That was the direction we were headed.

10

Slowly, I raised my foot from the brake. The Ford lurched and then settled, rolling across the parking lot. Puddles split under the Super Treadblasters as we waddled left then right. Mostly we stayed on the pavement.

As I crossed the curb something flashed in the rear-view mirror. Miss Jeannie, probably, orange head bob-bob-bobbing across the parking lot. Or was it Daddy chasing after us? No. Chasing after his Faithful Ford.

He'd jump into Ed's pickup and run us down, and . . .

I couldn't look. No turning back. We were off.

The Faithful Ford hummed down Main Street, happy to be my car. I leaned my elbow on its windowsill and steered with one hand. I'd found my true talent, car wrangler extraordinaire. I'd be a race-car driver, or open my own chain of driving schools—Margie Tempest Instant Automobile Academy: Hop In and Drive.

Or maybe I'd go into the rescue business, full-time. Lost dogs, lost cats, lost mommas.

"Take me home!" Peep shrieked, so loud the raindrops trembled on the window glass.

"Fine." If that's what she wanted, that's what she'd get. We'd cruise down Main Street, and when we passed friends and neighbors I'd wave. They'd see Margie Tempest behind the wheel. They'd know I was special.

But no one was out on the street in the rain. No old women walking dogs or old men trading stories. No kids racing bikes, popping wheelies under the streetlight. No one to show. No one to tell.

We turned left from Main onto Boone Avenue, swinging wide into the left lane. The Ford's steering wheel spun back, slipping smooth beneath my palms. Tires whirled. Engine lunged. Daddy's car didn't want to be controlled, but I made it behave. I tapped the brake, and we barely slowed, whizzing through intersections, whipping down Maple Street—oops! a little bit close to a minivan parked on the side of the road.

Don't do that again, Ford! Stay on the blacktop.

I was boss here.

Peep's shoulders were hunched under her ears. "Slow down!"

Chicken Peep. The sky wasn't falling. We'd ridden our bikes faster than this. But it *was* different in a car.

Auto-matic.

We slid through the intersection, past that big red stop sign, past Imp's Place and Fill 'R Up.

"Turn! Turn now!" Peep said, like she was the boss.

I twisted the wheel, and the tires began to screech. The Faithful Ford's rear end swung left—out—out— until the tires grabbed back hold of the blacktop.

"See?" she said.

I saw nothing but open road.

Freedom.

Peep wrapped the seat belt a couple more loops around her hand. Soon she'd cut off her circulation, for sure.

We were on Pine Street now, whizzing past the Madisons' and Mrs. Bell's. Their houses weren't the same through the Faithful Ford's windshield, me behind the wheel. They seemed far away, perched on their tiny rectangles of grass, like I was peering down from another galaxy.

"Our lights are on," Peep announced all happy as we rolled toward our house.

"We left them on," I said, and pushed right on past. Barely looking, I could tell Momma's car wasn't in the drive.

"Stop now, Margie!" Peep said.

"No," I said. "I'm on a mission." I hurried the Faithful Ford along, to the corner, around the curve, down the Fairdale hill. Tasty Yum flashed by on one side, Good Grace Church of the Redemption on the other. Peep pressed her palms together and started to pray.

Daddy was a churchgoing man, every Sunday. Then back for prayer meeting Wednesday night. Daddy and his Brave Souls pondered how to "Love thy neighbor," when your neighbor let the dandelions grow all summer, and they went from pretty yellow flowers to a field full of fluffy white seeds and ruined every scrap of that fescue you sowed, watered, cut, and trimmed. Or the great "Turn the other cheek" debate. Or the mystery of how many points the Simpkins boy would have shot if that referee from Edmonds hadn't fouled him out last Saturday night.

Those Psalm lambs were always losing their way, galloping down the wrong path, not like me, doing exactly right. But Daddy might not see it that way. At least not at first. A forgiving Bible verse would work wonders when he walked out to the World of Tires lot and saw his Faithful Ford missing. Those Brave Souls better have been practicing up on their prayers.

Another minute and we were on Bridge Street. I stepped hard on the gas and we flew right across.

Out of Ithaca.

Off the page.

Gone.

11

As soon as we crossed the bridge, Peep yanked out Daddy's *Roadways of the U.S.A.* from the glove compartment.

No.

No maps. No matter which route she picked, I was driving my own way. Daddy had a sense of direction and so did I. He never used a map. He'd press the gas and soon we'd be there, no problem, every single time. That's how I'd drive, too.

"Millersville Pike," Peep said.

"I know how to go."

"It's a left turn. In half a mile," she said.

I steered. I pushed the gas. I pretended she didn't bother me.

"What about gas?" Peep asked, like she was the driving boss of the map, the gas tank, everything.

Nope. Not in my car. I was in charge now.

But I pulled my eyes off the road and searched for the gas gauge—left, right, middle. Finally I found a tiny picture of a gas pump with a quivering green needle. "It says we have a quarter of a tank." How far that would get us was anybody's guess.

Peep didn't have to guess. She always knew the answer, even before you asked the question. "This car has a huge gas tank," she said. Little Miss AutoMart. "A hundred gallons at least, and a quarter of that is twenty-five." Like I didn't know my fractions. "And if we get fifteen miles to the gallon . . ." She paused, just how Miss Primrose did, to embarrass somebody into taking a guess.

I wasn't falling for that. Gallons and a quarter and miles per hour. All I cared about was if there was enough. We would get there. Correction. I would get us there.

I steered past the last lights from town, till mailboxes got real scarce. The road was twisty and dark, with teeny arcs of landscape lit in the headlights. Silhouettes flashed through the windows, across the dash, over the seat. A scraggly tree pointed its skeleton fingers down the road. *Run. Run. Run,* it said, then evaporated quick as we drew close. Like maybe there wasn't anything real beyond the Faithful Ford's hood, just a great black beyond. Like the whole wide world was me and Peep and the car, and we were headed off the edge, into the unknown. How did you draw *that* on a map?

"You passed Millersville Pike," Peep yelled, swiveling in her seat. "The turn was back there."

"I have a better plan."

"You're going to get us lost," she said, waving the map in my face, right in front of the windshield, so I couldn't see the road.

"Stop!" I yelled.

The Super Treadblasters groaned, skidding across the gravel shoulder. The Faithful Ford might be a good car, loyal and true, but it couldn't go in the right direction without somebody steering. And I couldn't steer if I couldn't see.

Peep shook the map again. "If you won't look at this—"

So I grabbed Daddy's atlas right out of her hand.

"Margie!" Peep shrieked, like I was the one doing something wrong.

It didn't take more than a second to get the Ford back on the road, steering and clutching the atlas with my right hand, and cranking the window down with my left.

"What are you doing?" Peep said. "You're going to get the car wet, and us lost, and—"

I didn't need to leave the window down for long. Soon as it was cracked to my shoulder I tossed that stupid book full of maps out and watched as it thumped across the pavement.

So long.

"What did you do? That's Daddy's atlas! You'll get us lost!"

Daddy wouldn't be too happy when he popped open the glove compartment and found it empty. No more *Roadways of the U.S.A.* No more stiff green case. No more . . . I was setting our course, not some printed up stack of pages. But for a second, just a split second, I wondered . . . NO. I did not need a map.

Peep didn't understand. I wasn't getting us lost. I was getting us found.

She got quiet, burrowed in on her side of the seat, and said just one more thing. "I hate you."

Fine. The feeling was mutual.

12

I would take the highway. The fast way. Momma was afraid to drive on the highway with all those trucks. Not me. We would get to Flench fast, pick up Momma, and be back by bedtime. Tonight Daddy worked closing at World of Tires. He'd be last out, locking the door behind him, and he'd never need to know that we'd left. Except he'd want to congratulate me on my new driving skills. He might give me my own key to the Ford.

I steered onto the entrance ramp. Full speed ahead.

Peep steamed the windows with her smoldering smarter-than-thou temper. I didn't care. I was the driver. Our route was up to me to decide.

The windshield wipers flapped and the wheels spun and the green hands on the clock said 6:32, then 7:14. My arms went stiff, my shoulders, too. Ten miles on, then twenty. Green road signs grew from the horizon like summer corn, soaring tall as we drove near. Grassy Creek and Pine Ridge, Decoy and Hazel Green. Soon I'd see the sign for Flench and I'd pull off and that would be all.

But the Faithful Ford didn't make it easy, teasing me with the gas needle, curtsying, dipping, hovering between one-eighth and the fat red E. We had plenty of gas, that's what Peep said, and she'd done the math. There must be a sticky gasket. A loose connection between the tank and that needle. We had enough gas. I was sure of it. But . . .

Did cars have alarms that announced they were on empty? *Whoop Whoop Whoop: Get off the road!* like the fire alarm at school? *Danger: Fill me up now!*

No. That was stupid. Peep said we had enough. She wasn't much of a sister, but she could multiply. We'd be fine.

"Daddy's off work by now," she said, staring out her side.

Thanks for the update, I thought, but didn't say.

I knew how it went. Daddy tallied his receipts and posted his daily sales form. He made sure the light was off out back and said good-night to Miss Jeannie. She said something about her TV shows, or the cute trick she was teaching her poodle. Then Ed locked the front door.

By now Daddy was in the parking lot.

Was he looking for his Faithful Ford, wondering if he'd forgot and left it home?

Was he worried?

Was he calling the police?

Did he care?

The wind picked up and branches rustled outside the windows. There were no more cars on the highway. Just us and the trees and the wind.

"We're lost," Peep said.

"No, we're not."

"Then where are we?" Peep asked.

Maybe I couldn't pinpoint our exact location this very second. That did not mean we were lost.

"You said the Flench exit was close," she said.

"It is close." We'd already gone miles and miles. It had to be close.

"You're driving in the wrong direction."

No. Peep was the one who was wrong. She didn't understand. My natural driving skills would get us there. No visual aids.

The Ford rolled on, up and down, over and around.

"I'm hungry," Peep said.

My stomach rumbled like it wanted to agree with her. "We'll be there soon," I said.

"But I'm hungry now."

Rumble. Rumble. Betrayer. "You should have eaten that soup," I said.

"I didn't know I was on death row and mushroom soup would be my last meal."

Little Miss Priss. I wasn't stopping to get her something to eat now. Not rewarding that smart mouth. Where'd she think we'd get money for food, anyway?

The Super Treadblasters hummed, and the gas gauge hovered, and the road rolled by.

```
Graville      7
Booneville   15
```

"You're going in the wrong direction," she said. "Flench is east of home. You're driving west. We'll never get there."

"Roads don't just go in one straight line," I said. And I'd picked the right direction, on the right road, probably.

```
Booneville   3
Le Rose      7
```

Towns flew past. Still no Flench.

"You know Cain in the Bible?" Peep said.

I gripped the steering wheel. What was she up to now? "You mean that Cain who killed his brother?"

"Yeah. After he did that he went out in the desert and

wandered around, same as this." She paused. I felt those blue laser eyes drill through me. "It was God's revenge."

"Right, it is the same," I agreed. "Except I haven't killed you yet."

That zipped her lips.

And okay, looking at a map might not have been a bad idea. One quick glimpse would have been nice. Just to prove I was right. Insurance, kind of. Peace of mind. But Daddy's atlas was somewhere a zillion miles back, soggy on the side of the road.

The sign said there was a rest stop up ahead, and rest stops had maps, great big ones mounted up on the wall. Maps I could peek at, nonchalant, on my way to the bathroom. Maps Peep would never notice I'd checked.

"I need to stretch my legs," I said as I steered the Faithful Ford to the exit ramp.

"You said we weren't stopping until we were in Flench."

"This isn't a stop. It's a pause."

"But—"

"I have to pee," I said.

She couldn't argue with that.

She folded her arms across her chest as I pulled up to a parking spot next to a little white car. "I'm not going in there," she said. "Momma says you get a rash in a place like that."

"You won't get a rash," I said, unclipping my seat belt.

"I'm still not going in there," Peep repeated.

"Suit yourself," I said, like she wasn't playing right into my hands.

The wet breeze whipped at Daddy's jacket—no, my jacket now. I stuffed my hands deep into the pockets, turning the Faithful Ford's key between my fingers.

Maybe throwing that atlas out the window hadn't been my smartest move, but I couldn't give Peep the upper hand. Peep could not be Queen of the Road. That title belonged to me.

The rest stop was spic-and-span clean inside, with bright shiny lights that cast a sort of green glow over the racks of cards that lined the walls. See Rock City! Pinnacle Overlook! Follow the Ridge to the Natural Bridge! I didn't care about any of that. Just that great big map, that was it. I glanced over my shoulder out the wall of windows. Peep was still in the car, watching me, no doubt. Watching my every move, to add it to her report once we got home.

You won't believe what Margie did next—after she threw out your atlas and made the car skid and hauled us into some rest stop that gave me a rash just looking through the window— I could hear her now. Then she'd go off on some wild tale, how I'd asked strangers for directions or stolen the map right off the wall or who knows what.

There were people in the lobby area. Loitering. A woman looked up from a rack of brochures. *Mind your own business,* I almost said. But I didn't need to tell her. Her chin had already tilted back down. Her eyes had already shifted to the flyer for the Candyland Motel, or the Endless Waters, or the Authentic Indian Village.

A man stood next to her, with a little girl tugging at his pants leg. The girl's eyes were tired and grumpy. I could just imagine what it was like riding in that car: little girl whining, kicking the back of the seat; Momma up front, pointing out every boring site; Daddy trying his best to drive, even though the other two had given him a splitting headache.

That's how it was with families.

"How much longer, Daddy?" the little girl asked, like a mini-version of Peep. *Hush your griping,* I thought he'd snap, or *We'll get there when we get there.* Or he'd ignore her. Whatever it took to shut her up.

"Just an hour more," he said, oh so soft. "Here, let me show you." He picked the kid up and held her to the great big map on the wall, the one I was supposed to be studying. Hogging it, standing right up in front of it so I could barely see.

"Here we are, baby," the man said, pointing to a big

red dot in the lower right corner. "And this is where we're going." He took the little girl's hand in his, pointing her finger, tracing it across the roads. "The blue road, to the red one, to the green one."

He smiled and she smiled and I frowned.

"Excuse me," I said. "I need to check something."

"Surely," the man said, stepping aside, like some Mr. Nice Guy.

That big red dot—that YOU ARE HERE—was completely in the wrong place.

Nowhere near where I thought we were.

Nowhere near Flench.

My stomach went sour. Peep had been right. I'd driven the wrong direction. We had to go back ten, no, twenty miles. Then get off the highway. Where? Route 6 left. Then a little way north to State Road 16 and . . . I was never going to remember this.

"Would you like a drink, baby?" the woman said.

The little girl nodded and the man carried her to the water fountain. How cute. How caring. How totally stupid for me to stand here looking at those people when I needed to be memorizing the way back to Flench.

Route 6, State Road 16, left then right, north then east. Roads I'd never seen, ones I didn't remember, all laid out in a great big tangle. No way I'd ever remember them all. We'd be stuck on the road forever, just like Peep said. Wanderers.

"Do you have a pen?" I asked.

The man and woman looked up, like they were surprised I was standing there, like I'd been invisible until this second. "A pen," I repeated. "Do you have a ballpoint pen I can borrow for just a second?"

"Why does that little girl want a pen?" the kid asked.

I was *not* a little girl. Even Miss Primrose didn't call me little. But I held my tongue while the woman shushed her daughter and dug through her purse, handing me a cheap plastic pen.

Daddy gave way nicer pens out at World of Tires. Free. For promotional purposes. And he . . .

Forget Daddy.

"Thanks," I mumbled, and traced the roads on the big wall map with my finger, just like the man had done with his daughter, showing her the way.

Then I opened my palm and pushed the ballpoint tip to my skin, tracing my own map onto my flesh. A quick jog left for Route 6, then a long, windy streak that ran along my life line. Left, right, zigzags, the ballpoint etched its way to Momma. To where we'd be a family again.

Up, down, all around. Keep on driving and you'll get there, someday. Maybe. If you're lucky. My mistakes and do-overs, tattooed onto my palm.

I handed back the pen and glanced over my shoulder as I pushed out the door. Those people weren't watching. Who was I? Just some weird kid who wrote on herself. What did they care? What did anybody care?

"I thought of a shortcut," I said, swinging the car door open.

A cloud of sweet poured from the car, thick as smoke. Peep was stiff in her seat, lips pursed.

"What have you been doing?" I asked.

"Nothing," she mumbled, lips clamped shut, but the dark smudges around her mouth betrayed her.

"Open your mouth."

"No," she said, muffled, glaring at me, eyes lowered in shame like a bad dog who'd been caught in the garbage.

I couldn't stop my stomach from growling. The whole car stunk like candy. Chocolate.

Seconds ticked by. Finally she spoke. "I was hungry."

I pulled my seat belt and snapped it in place.

"I didn't do anything wrong," she said.

I put the key in the ignition and twisted it.

"You lied and kidnapped me," she said.

I slipped the gear lever into reverse.

"It was my A+ money," she said.

The Faithful Ford backed from the parking spot, careful.

"There wasn't enough for you," she said.

13

I pulled back onto the highway. The other way.

All that chocolate had glued Peep's lips shut. Peace at last.

But quiet meant space inside my head. Space to notice how that broken white line wound down the center of the road, chopped, like slices of my old copperhead . . .

I'd wanted to carry that snake to school. I'd keep him in a shoe box, all day long. I wouldn't show off, touching those needle-sharp teeth. Not for anybody. Not even for Jimmy. Promise.

Jimmy would notice me all right. He'd say "Killer!" and the rest of the kids would say "Coooool."

But Daddy said no snake, and Momma went along. She put him in the trash, wound inside two plastic bags. That was that.

They thought.

I woke up early, before the garbage trucks came, and I pulled the bag out of the can at the end of the driveway, and slid my copperhead into my backpack, and carried him to school, snake head, snake tail, and all the parts. It didn't even stink. Yet.

I felt Peep's eyes boring into me, all the way across the classroom. After the first week, Miss Primrose knew better than to seat us side by side. I turned, casual, and gave her a squint-eyed drop-dead glare and she withered into the background.

Now I was free to slip my snake out to recess. The playground was cold and gray and shivery and it looked like rain, but I didn't mind. I had my snake.

"Look at my copperhead," I said.

None of the girls would even peek, but the boys clustered around. Jimmy noticed. Me. Me and my snake.

"I hunted it down," I said. "I killed it, too."

Jimmy opened the sack and his mouth gaped into a big round O. Then Warren Marshall took one glance and said, "Margie's a liar. That's nothing but an old milk snake. Harmless."

Jimmy looked away, taking a step back, staring at his tennis shoes.

I wasn't any liar. I'd found that snake. Milk snake? Copperhead? Who cared? They looked the same. And I *had* killed it, sort of. Had it killed anyway. What did it matter?

But it did matter.

Everything mattered.

A lot.

Jimmy wandered off, then the other kids, too. Peep even. And Miss Primrose sent me to detention.

Class disrupter.

Liar, liar, pants on fire.

Where did I think I was living?

In some dream world?

Couldn't I tell a lie from the truth?

14

Soon as we got to the right road the rain started up again, first one, then two drops, then a torrent.

"There are 50 percent more automobile accidents in the rain," Peep said.

"Thanks for the information." Who cared about that 50 percent? It wouldn't be the Faithful Ford that slid off the road, not with me behind the wheel. I was glad of the rain, glad to concentrate, squinty-eyed, on the clear patch through the windshield. Relieved to hear the muffled roar of raindrops and wipers that filled the prickly silence.

"The majority of wrecks result in at least one fatality," she said.

She called me a liar, but she was the one with made-up specifics, designed to scare me and make her sound smart. We were not going to crash and croak. We were on the right road now. I had it all under control. But my foot eased off the gas, just in case.

Tree after tree washed by the windows, gnarled and scrubby, winding between fence posts and tangles of barbed wire. It seemed like there was nothing in the whole wide world but endless dark and road.

For a second, a split second, my eyes dropped from the windshield's smeary glass to the gas gauge. That cute little gas pump, the one that looked like an elf's toy? It showed a quarter of a tank when we left. "Plenty," Peep had said. Twenty-five gallons. Then it was one-eighth. Now it had dropped.

A lot.

The needle bobbed then curtsied deep. E . . . E . . . E. I didn't need Peep to translate. Even I knew E stood for empty.

"There must be something wrong with Daddy's car," I said. "The needle on the gas gauge is real low."

"We should have plenty of gas. You must have broken it."

"I didn't break anything," I said.

"Then the needle's stuck," she said. "You better be going the right way, *this time*," she added, even though I hadn't mentioned our slight change of course.

This time I'd aimed us, like an arrow, straight for Momma. I *was* doing right. Couldn't she see?

Momma would let out a squeal when me and Peep got there. She'd set down her canisters and give us a hug. Even though I didn't hug. Even though Momma didn't hug either. She'd say she'd had enough of chickens, and we'd be home in time for bed.

The road twisted and twined, time and space flashing by. It wouldn't be much longer now.

Then without even a whisper of warning the Faithful Ford lunged, striking like that copperhead, slithering right and left, dodging my hands on the steering wheel.

No, Ford. I'm the boss.

But it refused to listen. Was it remembering it was Daddy's car?

"Margie! Stop it!" Peep screamed, like I was putting on a show.

Trees whipped past the windshield, blurred, there and gone.

Don't look. Don't look. Eyes on the clock. The speedometer. The gas gauge. The ditch as the Un-Faithful Ford spun,

around,

and around,

and around.

Guts and heart and lungs twisted inside me. Peep's spare dimes orbited my head.

Skidding . . . skidddddding . . . skidddddddddd dddding . . . Until we stopped. Dead. End.

15

So that was how a car ran out of gas. The Ford sat on the side of the road and I wanted a do-over. Just one.

If I had one do-over this is what it would be: I would not listen to Peep. I would not believe her big-brain not-real math facts on how many miles you could drive with one quarter of a tank of gasoline. I would yank every one of those dimes from Peep's fat little fist and pump the Faithful Ford full of gas before we rolled out of Ithaca. When Peep talked I would shut my ears, like Daddy when I tried to explain what went wrong at school. I would not listen to Peep. I WOULD NOT LISTEN TO ANYONE BUT MYSELF.

That was not all. If I had one do-over, I would go to the beginning of today. No, farther back. Yesterday or the day before that. I would go as far back as do-overs went.

Before Peep was born, maybe.

I would get everything right next time.

When I was little, me and Marsha Pendleton and all the other kids played in the road, till way past twilight. The lightning bugs came out, all of them, not just those early birds who flew around shiny and confused in the afternoon. Those bugs flashed like a hundred strings of Christmas lights.

We played freeze tag and hide-and-seek in the dark. Peep begged till we let her play, too. Even though she was too little and too scared of the dark and too whiny and too everything but fun. Even though I didn't want her here or there or anywhere. Even though all she wanted to play was Mother, May I. The rest of them said yes. Not me.

"Mother, may I take three giant steps?"

"Yes, you may."

I stretched my long legs, handy for a change, right across the road. Right to the Madisons' yard. To the mulberry weed tree that nearly strangled their mailbox. Black-red fruit hung in heavy clumps, dropping when branches rustled. Junk fruit, Daddy called it.

The berries littered the street in purple puddles, and I giant-stepped right on top of them, screwing my feet into the pavement, dyeing the soles of my tennis shoes bloody black and blue. I didn't care that Daddy would say, "Marjorie Ann, those shoes cost me good money. What do you have to say for yourself?" The squish felt good, like an accomplishment.

"Mother, may I hop four times?" Marsha yelled.

"Yes, you may."

And she jumped, *Hop Hop Hop Hop,* like a bullfrog throwing a fit.

Then Jimmy McDonald, eyes flashing like his own personal pair of lightning bugs, had his turn. He leaped across the road, graceful as a boy deer.

I was the mother when Peep asked, "Can I take thirteen baby steps?" She thought she'd look cute, mincing across that blacktop. I knew she had it calculated, mathematically. Five-year-old weirdo, using math to beat me. Each baby step eight inches, so eight times thirteen is . . . a lot. One hundred four or one hundred six or something, almost nine feet. Practically the whole circumference, or area, or whatever, across the entire street.

Peep could not fool me.

"No, you may not," I said.

But Peep wouldn't listen. She was off in her own time warp, baby-stepping across the road—one, two, three, four—every inch measured out just right.

But I screamed: "You're out. You didn't say 'Mother, may I?' No do-overs!"

All the way back to the starting line.

There was no such thing as a do-over. Not in real life. There were just mistakes. And my mistakes came back around again and again, no matter how hard I tried to move on.

I studied the lines on my palm and racked my brain. What else did the map at that rest stop show? What had that daddy's finger traced? "There's a town, Graville, about a mile up the road."

"We don't have money for gas," Peep said.

I picked one of her dimes off the seat. "We'd have plenty if you hadn't stuffed yourself full of chocolate."

Her lip bulged but she wasn't getting any sympathy from me. "My dimes wouldn't have been enough. All I carry with me is two A+'s worth. Two dollars."

"There are five dimes here on the seat. How many more in your pocket?"

Peep pulled two crumpled candy wrappers from her pocket, trying to sneak them, but she couldn't fool me. Then the money. She dropped three dimes in my outstretched palm: *Clink Clink Clink.* "That's not enough for a gallon of gas."

"Open the glove compartment," I said.

"Why?"

"Just do it."

And for once, Peep didn't fuss.

I leaned across her and pulled a tapestry coin purse from the back.

"That's not yours," she said.

I popped the rusty snap open. Inside were six dollar bills and some coins.

"You're stealing," Peep said. "It's Daddy's mad money. For emergencies."

"What do you think this is?" We were stranded on the side of the road with a dead car. This wasn't just an emergency. This was a disaster. I unbuckled my seat belt and opened the car door.

"I'm not going with you, spending Daddy's and my money to run a stolen car," Peep snipped.

"I don't care what you do," I said, climbing out. The rain had let up some, but I zipped the jacket to the top. I opened the trunk and found Daddy's gas can, nestled in the back corner. He'd never used it and never would. Daddy didn't run out of gas. Jimmy wouldn't run out of gas either. But I needed that can. I had run Daddy's Faithful Ford bone dry.

No. This was Peep's fault. Even if they'd all hold me accountable.

"Watch out for snakes," I called over my shoulder as I headed out.

"Wait!" Chicken Peep said as she sprang out of the car. "You're walking the wrong way!"

I stopped.

"Margie?"

I paused. One do-over. I turned and began to walk the other way. And Peep followed.

16

"You're lucky to have me," Peep called up to me, quieter without her dime payload. "'Cause I can show you the way."

I didn't answer.

"We can call Daddy at the gas station," Peep said, like she was trying out the idea, probably thinking I'd jump right on it.

Call Daddy? Admit I'd failed? Again? She could forget that. I shifted to hyper-speed.

He wasn't coming to our rescue. He'd had his chance. Now it was up to me. And the last thing I needed was Daddy finding the Ford on the side of the road. Peep wouldn't be the one who took the blame.

Peep scampered along, keeping up no matter how fast I walked, like she thought if we walked together we'd be on the same team. News flash. We weren't friends. We

were just hitched one to the other, a pair of escaped crimi-
nals locked together in handcuffs.

My feet clip-clopped down the road and I tried to
settle on a plan for how I could fix this. But dark thoughts
rolled across my mind instead, heavier than the storm
clouds overhead. More threatening, too.

Jimmy McDonald would never run out of gas, driving.
Two reasons:

1) Jimmy would not be dumb enough to listen
to Peep. At school, when Peep's hand popped up
ten, fifteen, twenty times an hour, Miss Primrose
kept calling on her, just encouraging her. Jimmy
and the other boys went from rolling their eyes to
groaning to rolling pencils up and down the aisles.
Peter Watson shot spit wads. If Jimmy and the
other boys didn't listen to Peep when she blabbed
on about Panama's corn crop and how to avoid
dangling modifiers, no way Jimmy would listen to
what she said about gasoline.

2) Jimmy didn't have to figure out gas or directions or anything else when he drove. Jimmy hadn't
been alone in that car, whipping down the road
ninety miles an hour. He had his daddy right beside him, showing him the way.

So . . . That should teach me a lesson. Peep didn't know it all. Not by a long shot.

All I had was me. I wouldn't rely on anyone else, not ever again.

Finally, something appeared over the hill. A cluster of buildings squatted on the side of the road, with a great big half-rusted sign out front.

Al's Pump 'n Dine.

Gas.

I exhaled. How long had I been holding my breath? Ten minutes, at least. I should have timed myself for the record books: Amazing Purple Girl Hikes Without Air, Drags Crabby Sister Along.

When we got closer I could see Al's wasn't exactly clean and tidy. Prime territory for giving you a rash. Momma would have had her sponge out.

"Wait here," I said as I carried the gas can to the pump. But, surprise, Peep pushed past me. Her shadow slipped behind her like a dark ghost hurrying to catch up, hovering over the cracked blacktop, shimmering blue and pink as it crossed the greasy puddles.

"Don't you dare call Daddy!" I yelled, but she slammed the streaky glass door against my nose, charging through to the bathroom.

Fine. She'd be safe in there. What trouble could she get into?

Al could have won a prize for running the world's filthiest gas station, with grease and mud and a hundred years of dirt caking the floor. The air was heavy with the stink of motor oil and whining radio music. An attendant behind the counter, hair as black as skunk fur, looked up from a bride magazine. "Facilities are for customers only."

Take it slow and grownup, I told myself. "I . . . we *are* customers," I said. "I need eight dollars and forty-three cents' worth of gas."

She glanced at me, jaw slack, and flipped a page with the end of her long red fingernail.

She knew. I could see it in her dull tannish eyes, lined with thick black stripes of mascara. She could tell I was a twelve-year-old car thief. And she could tell I'd kidnapped my sister, and broken Jimmy McDonald's ankle. Okay, not Jimmy McDonald's ankle, specifically, but she could tell I was dangerous. And crazy.

But I couldn't run. Peep was locked in the bathroom. There was no gas in the Ford. All I could do was face her. And lie.

"My mom's with the car," I said.

She flipped to an ad for miniature brides and grooms to stick on the tops of cakes.

"We ran out of gas," I said.

Silence.

"That's why you don't see a car out there, because we didn't make it all the way before we ran out of gas," I said. "But I have a can. For the gas."

She flicked to the next page, faking like she wasn't interested. "That kid better not be sick in my bathroom."

I was the one who was about to be sick. "My sister had to pee," I said. "That's all. That's why Mom sent me, to take her to the bathroom. While she waits in the car." I threw the money on the counter, coins muffled by the wrinkled dollars. Three of the dimes rolled into the chewing gum rack. I fished them out and plunked them on top of the rest. "I want the cheapest gas. Here's eight dollars and forty-three cents."

Skunk-hair rolled her mean cat eyes and scratched at the change with her talons. "Pump 1," she said.

I didn't move.

"This ain't full service," she said.

Right.

It was still drizzly outside but I didn't care. I'd pump the gas fast and get back on the road. I still had that map scratched onto my palm: a skinny river of blue ballpoint, left and right, tracing the lines of my hand. It was smudged, from my sweaty palm rubbing along the steering wheel. But it was all there. I'd get this gas and rush back to the car and I'd make it.

Tough on Peep if she couldn't keep up.

There were three flavors of gas: blue, red, and white. White was the cheapest. The Faithful Ford better like it. I pulled the hose, stinky and black with oil, and stuffed it into the gas can and I squeezed the handle for all I was worth. Gas shot out like a geyser, spraying my jeans, the pump, the gas can, everything. Smellier than all the sixth-grade boys at Jesse Stuart Elementary rolled into one.

But that wasn't the worst thing. It was seventy-three cents wasted. Not a drop of gas in the can.

I started again. Slow. Gentle. Hold the nozzle. Put it in the can. Squeeze. The gas can gulped like a hungry baby. Three glugs, and it had swallowed the whole $8.43, minus what it had spit up on me.

I hung the nozzle up and still no Peep. What was she doing in there all this time? How long did it take to go to the bathroom? Pants down. Tinkle. Pants up. Hand washing optional.

I could leave her now. I had the gas. But on her own there was no telling the trouble she'd cause.

Headlights flashed across my legs just as I started for

the door. So what? This was a gas station. Of course there were other cars, other drivers who needed a tank of gas.

I pushed inside, glancing over my shoulder as I slipped through the door. My blood turned to icy slush in one second flat.

The car was two-toned, silver and blue, with big yellow words on the door.

The police were here.

For me.

17

When Miss Jeannie waited on soldiers at the World of Tires, or watched the Flood County marching band in the Fourth of July parade, or stood in line at the Happy Hamburger, even, she'd say, "There's something about a man in uniform," loud enough for everybody to hear. Then she'd sigh. Which made no sense. People dressed alike were just head-to-toe boring as far as I was concerned.

But when I saw the man who climbed from the car by the gas pumps I understood. He must have been eight feet tall, with a smashed-up nose that said he wasn't afraid to fight. A pair of legs thick as tree trunks, and shoulders like a bull. But it was his uniform that sealed it, stern gray except for his wide black belt, jingling with handcuffs. A sharp-edged silvery hat. A shiny badge. A gun.

There *was* something about that man in uniform.

Something real scary.

I pushed inside the station, quick.

"That kid's still in the toilet," Skunk-hair yelled from behind her magazine.

She'd done it. Skunk-hair must have called that policeman on me, for underage gas pumping. On Peep for excessive bathroom use.

I peered around a grocery shelf through the dirty plate-glass window. The trooper had pulled a squeegee from a tank of gray watery stuff that hung beside the pump. He scraped the squeegee across the cruiser's windshield and polished the glass with a paper towel.

Who cleaned their windows in the rain? No. He was stalling for time. Waiting for backup before he made the arrest.

"Peep!"

No answer.

Her dawdling was going to get us both thrown in jail.

I ran down the aisle and peered, between canned beef stew and Vienna sausages, out the smudgy window. He pulled the gas hose from his tank and hung it back on the pump, pretending not to notice my gas can on the ground. Pretending. Police were trained to notice everything.

Skunk-hair sat calm, blowing bubbles big as cats' heads, and popping them with her pinky nail, waiting for the show to begin when that trooper slapped the handcuffs on me and threw me in the car.

You have the right to remain silent. Just remember that.

But Peep would blab it all.

"Hurry," I said to the door, not even trying to whisper now.

The trooper walked slowly across the pavement and opened the station door, beating the rain off his sleeves with the back of his hand.

For a second I wondered if Peep was okay. Maybe she'd fainted or had an attack of some kind.

No. She was doing this on purpose. It was just like her, holed up in that bathroom, me out here trembling. She could probably see me through the keyhole. She was probably laughing her head off.

The trooper trailed greasy puddles across the linoleum and my heart counted every step. He unzipped his jacket, handcuffs clanking against his belt. I could feel their cold metal around my wrists.

"Peep!"

"Something going on in that restroom?" Skunk-hair yelled.

"We're fine," I called in my most grownup voice.

The trooper pawed through the chocolate bars, then leaned his elbow on the checkout counter. Casual-like. But he couldn't fool me. He was lying in wait, counting the seconds, ready to pounce.

Finally, the ladies' room door creaked open, and Peep sauntered into the light, fine and dandy, like she hadn't kept me out here waiting for a year and a half.

Then I saw it . . .

in the ladies room . . .

by the Ready Squirt Perfume Dispenser . . .

a pay phone.

18

All of a sudden the trooper was the least of my worries. I grabbed Peep's elbow and dragged her behind the chips.

Her eyes darted around all shifty and her arms clamped tight to her sides. No matter what she said, I wasn't completely stupid. I knew what she'd been doing in the bathroom so long. She was on that phone, calling Daddy. He was on his way. I was about to get caught.

"I told you not to do it," I said.

Peep clenched her jaw. "I don't know what you're talking about."

Her? Admit she didn't know something? Amazing.

"Do you see the policeman over there?" I asked.

The trooper seemed so ordinary, leaning toward the register, pouring coffee into a Styrofoam cup. But his hat and his badge had their effect. Peep went pale.

"I should have left you here," I said.

Peep stuck her bottom lip out, a baby ready for her tantrum. "You can't blame me because—"

"What do you think that trooper will do when Daddy gets here?" I said, quieter this time. "What will he say when he finds out Daddy let two little kids drive his car?"

"He didn't let you drive. You stole—"

"Daddy waved me out to his car. He as good as invited me to use it."

Peep shifted like she didn't know whether to fight me or the trooper, or just run back into that bathroom and lock herself in.

"He'll slap those handcuffs on, quick as a wink," I said. "He'll toss Daddy in jail and throw away the key, for raising a pair of juvenile delinquents."

"You're the juvenile delinquent," Peep said, way too loud.

The trooper looked up from his coffee. She had done it now.

"It isn't Daddy's fault," she whispered, fast and urgent.

"It will be *your* fault," I said. "Soon as Daddy gets here."

Peep's chin trembled. "You're so nasty. I didn't do anything wrong. I didn't talk to Daddy."

I narrowed my eyes and looked hard into hers. "You promise?"

Peep nodded.

"You swear on Momma and Daddy and Jesse Stuart Elementary?"

She looked at her shoes. "Swearing is wrong."

"Say it," I said.

"I promise," she said. "I swear on Miss Primrose, even."

Peep might have been a smarty-pants and a sneak, but she was no liar. She was so honest it would make a normal kid sick. So if she said she didn't call Daddy I believed her. "We've got to get out of here. Right now."

Peep nodded for a third time, and for once she did what I said, without any arguments, moving one step, then two.

"That restroom better be okay," Skunk-hair said as I shoved Peep toward the door.

"It's fine. Thank you so much," Peep said, smiling, standing up straight, like good manners would get her out of this mess.

Wrong.

I pushed her out the door, pulling her through the parking lot, grabbing the gas can on my way. It stunk and it was way heavy, bouncing against my leg, yanking my arm nearly out of joint. But I didn't mind. I had what I needed. Now my only choice was to run.

19

Hold up," Peep griped. "I can't walk that fast."

But I wasn't slowing down for anybody, least of all the creep.

Pavement gave way to mud on the road's shoulder and my tennis shoes squished a steady beat. I could hear the tippy-tap of her cute little feet but I didn't look back. No time. No need.

The Faithful Ford was waiting patiently where we left it. Peep hopped in while I fed gas into the tank. The Ford sucked it down, greedy, and quick as I could throw the can in the trunk we were ready to hit the road. The car started with a happy purr, not holding the running out of gas against me. A twist of the key, a push on the pedal, and we were off.

Peep didn't say a word. She knew better.

We'd gone a mile or two, faster and faster, Treadblasters

slicing the puddles, spinning like supersonic tops, when I noticed two pinpricks of light in the rearview mirror. They copied our every turn. "Someone's following us," I said, like the guy in a spy movie.

It was probably the trooper. The police could chase me, but they'd never take me. I'd be like Jesse James and Al Capone and all those guys, outrunning the law. I punched the gas and we surged, but car chases weren't so easy in real life, not like on the TV. We bounced and jolted, barely hanging on to the pavement.

"You're going too fast," Peep whimpered.

"Mind your own business," I said. But images of Bonnie and Clyde and Pretty Boy Floyd skidded into my head, folks who led the police on a merry chase but didn't end up so good. So I did slow down, just enough.

Speed or no speed, Peep loosened her seat belt and turned to the back for a better look. I should have quoted her how 12 percent of people not wearing seat belts fly through the windshield. She would have done that if it was me.

"There's no siren," she said. "I don't think it's police back there."

I peeked fast at the mirror. The lights were closer, coming on strong. "If it's not the trooper, who is it?"

"That looks like Ed's red truck."

"It can't be Ed." There was no reason . . . Unless that had been Daddy running after us back in the World of Tires parking lot. Unless he was . . .

Peep's voice went itsy-bitsy. "I have a confession," she said, melting back into her seat.

I gripped the wheel, glancing at those pinpoints of light in the rearview mirror, closer with every tick of the Faithful Ford's clock. Now did not seem such a great time for confessions.

"I told you something that wasn't exactly true."

The Ford jolted over a pothole as two thoughts criss-crossed my brain.

Number One: Stop the presses! Miss Perfect Admits a Lie. I never thought I'd see the day.

But right away it was canceled out by thought Number Two: What did Peep lie about? I had a sick feeling I already knew the answer.

"It was just misleading, not a lie," she said.

I'd mislead her, all right, mislead her off the side of the road, into a ditch. I punched the gas harder but those lights still hung on our tail, stalking, just far enough back.

"There was a pay phone inside that bathroom."

"I saw it," I said, clenching the steering wheel double-tight.

"I did call home," she said, her voice shaking even without potholes. "So I'm pretty sure that's Ed's truck back there. Daddy must have borrowed it. That's Daddy back there."

Breathe.

"How did you call if you didn't have money?"

Peep sat still and peaceful. Like she wasn't the world's biggest brat and a dirty rotten liar. "I dialed zero," she said. "I told the operator I was lost and I needed to talk to my daddy and she connected me for free."

"You what?" I said. "You talked to a stranger about us? You told her—"

"I had to," she said, twisting the seat belt around her hand, five, ten, fifteen times.

The only sounds were the Treadblasters chopping down the wet pavement, and my breathing hot and jaggy, and my heart booming, loudest of all.

"I needed to talk to Daddy," Peep said finally. "'Cause you have his car. So he can't come get us on his own and . . ." Peep was rambling, hysterical, sort of. But not the funny kind of hysterical. The crazy, nervous kind. She'd called, and Daddy was behind us, and probably the police back there, too. And now she was scared. And somehow this was all *my* fault.

"You better pull over," Peep said. "Daddy's fast."

Daddy was fast, all right. Fast to huff and puff and run us down. But it wasn't me he was after. He was looking for his precious Peep, the one who'd called him on the phone, begging, "Please oh please, come to my rescue."

Go, Ford, go. Run. The Super Treadblasters did their best, slapping through the puddles, hugging the curves, spinning faster, faster. But I'd had my driving debut only four hours before and holding the car on the road was easier said than done. Maybe Jimmy had gone ninety miles an hour, a hundred if the speedometer hadn't been broken, but I couldn't go that fast on my own.

And Daddy was fast. Too fast.

Finally, I knew, even without looking in the mirror, that the truck was right behind us. The square headlights rounded the bend on our tail, slow, not chasing anymore. Just following, settling in for the kill.

So I took my foot off the gas. Let it take us. Let it happen. Get it over with. Now.

The truck shifted to the left lane then drew next to us, door to door, spitting distance from the Faithful Ford. It was shiny blue, as bright as the sky at noon or a lake in August. As bright blue as Pretty Peep's eyes.

Not red like Ed's truck.

Not silver like the trooper's cruiser.

Not golden as a yolk, like the Faithful Ford, or blustery purple like Daddy's face when he was mad, mad, mad.

Then it nosed ahead, and *whooooooooooooooooosh*, that bright blue truck was gone.

I should have been relieved, sighing, and smiling, and glad. But that's not how my insides felt. My guts were jumbled. There was no relief.

"I guess I was wrong," Peep said quietly.

"Why'd you lie about calling him?"

"It wasn't a lie." Peep let her breath out slow, controlled, like blowing through a straw. "I called but I didn't talk to him. He didn't answer, so I left a message."

HE DIDN'T ANSWER?

Almost as bad as I HAVE TO GO.

"Of course he didn't answer," I said. Didn't Daddy give me that head shake, back at World of Tires? Didn't he shoot me that "Not now" look? And that "Go away" wave?

Daddy was way too busy reading *Tire and Radiator* to pick up the phone. Too busy filling out bonus reports, and climbing to the top of the World of Tires. *Daddy didn't answer because he doesn't have time for the likes of us,* I wanted to say.

No.

Daddy had time for Peep. He'd put down those papers and admire her grades any day, no matter that the inventory count was due last week and his accessory sales levels were lagging behind. He'd ooh and aah over Peep's work. He'd dig in his pocket and pass her a handful of A+ dimes, like they were peanuts.

Daddy not answering Peep's call was a mistake. He must have thought it was me on the line. And let the phone ring, ring, ring right off the hook. He let the machine pick up the call while he walked away.

I didn't deserve a glance, or a peanut, or one thin dime.

20

I shivered, but not from cold. There was no time for crying, out here on the road. No time to feel sorry for myself, when Momma was waiting. Daddy didn't care. So what?

"I'm sorry," Peep said.

"What?"

"I'm sorry I called Daddy. You said don't and I didn't listen and . . ."

"It's all right," I said. "It doesn't matter."

I wanted to drive. Just drive. Get there and be done. But Peep wanted to talk.

"What's it going to look like?" Peep asked.

"What?"

"That Poultry Hall of Fame. Where Momma went. What will it look like?"

I sat up straighter and squared my shoulders. "It will

be beautiful. White marble walls. Big columns. They'll have movies about chickens playing all the time so the tourists can come and go."

Peep nodded.

"There will be tours, and you'll have to mind your manners. No touching in a museum."

"Right."

I knew all about museums, on account of our fifth-grade field trip to the Museum of Natural History. Peep missed out, skipping through the grades, but she'd find out now, between the Hens of Distinction and the Hall of Roosters and . . .

"Momma will be there, waiting for us. Right?" she asked.

"Right." And that was all she needed to know.

The road was darker now, black and twisty as a licorice whip. I showed Peep the map inked on my hand and we followed that course, mindless, obedient to the steps.

Route 6 left.

A little way north.

Turn right on State Road 16.

My heart had gone hard, cold as a pebble rattling around in my chest. Daddy didn't care.

Forget it.

So what if—

What if I found Momma and we didn't go back home?

We'd drop Peep off, sliding to a quick stop outside the house, practically shoving her out of the car. No way she could go with us. She couldn't leave Miss Primrose and all those A+'s. She'd miss being Daddy's Pretty Little Princess.

But me and Momma didn't have those ties. We were free. We'd haul off on a nationwide chicken tour, piling Henny Penny and the hens in the car, rolling down to Georgia, to Marietta's Big Chicken. Then we'd set off for the Blue Hens in Delaware. San Diego and Rhode Island. Across the oceans, too. Famous chickens of Russia. China. Who knows? We wouldn't come home until we were good and ready. Until we were done.

This was a plan I didn't have to write on my hand.

Flench crept up slow, one house, then a gas station, then there it was.

> **Flench, Kentucky**
> **Population 1,347**

That would be 1,348 if you added Momma. She had driven down this very road not so long ago, tapping her brakes at this corner, flicking her blinker on, then turning right at exactly this spot. Her hens were next to her, strapped in tight. "How 'bout this, Clucky Lucky?" she must have said. "Ready to go to town?" Now I was following in her footsteps.

The deeper we burrowed into Flench the tighter Peep balled herself up, knees under her chin, skirt pulled across her legs like a wilted balloon. "This place isn't right," she said.

"You saw the sign, plain as day," I said. "It's Flench. We're here."

"It feels wrong," she said, tugging her skirt tighter, so hard it threatened to tear in two.

Chicken Peep.

This was right. Momma was here. I'd done it.

The Faithful Ford slunk down the street, past a dusty store that didn't seem to sell anything but broken furniture. Through the one stoplight. Slow. Look both ways. By a greasy-looking place called Cindy's Big Sip.

Everything was silent. There was no breeze, no crickets, not even raindrops pitter-pattering on the windshield. Even the Faithful Ford's motor hardly made a sound. It was almost quiet enough to hear my thoughts, so I hummed, tuneless, to shut them out.

Peep asked a question and for a second I was glad just to hear a sound. Then I realized what she'd asked. "Where's Momma?" The words hit hard, like a hammer breaking my rocky heart into gravel.

Momma wasn't here. Nobody was. Not a soul. If we drove around this town, lap on lap on lap, a hundred times around, not one person would know we'd been here. "It's too late for people," I said, like that answered anything.

Peep wound the seat belt another four or five times around her hand. "I want Momma," she said. "Now." Like that was big news.

"We'll go to the chicken museum," I said. "She's probably there." She'd be right inside the entrance, by the Hens of Distinction exhibit. She'd smile big when she saw us. We'd all rest easy.

Our map didn't show the roads inside town, and people who drove here were supposed to know where stuff was already. No foreigners allowed.

Up and down and back and forth, we drove until Peep spotted the sign. Bright and clear, a red-and-white metal vision from heaven, pointing the way.

Right on La Rope

Left on Spring

Hens and roosters led us.

Spring Street was full of potholes. From all the heavy traffic. Chicken fans. Cars and trucks, big tour buses, too, rolling in and out. In an endless stream, I bet. All those tires took a toll on blacktop. And, according to Daddy, all that blacktop took a toll on tires. That's what kept food on our table.

The Faithful Ford hopped and bounced to the end of the street. Down. Down. Down to the dead end.

"It's not here," Peep said. "There's no museum."

The International Poultry Hall of Fame had evaporated. But we'd seen the sign. There had to be a reasonable explanation. I just couldn't think of it.

Then Peep said, "Look!" and pointed at a short building huddled on the right side of the road. Painted letters peeled from the concrete block walls, words fainter still in the moonlight.

INT NAT L PO LTRY HAL OF FAME

No white columns. No mirrored walls. Just blistered wood and concrete.

We were here.

21

You'd think Peep would be happy, celebrating how I'd got us to Flench, found the Hall of Fame, and delivered us to the doorstep all in one piece. But noooooooooo. "Where is Momma?" she asked.

"She'll be here," I said. Then, "I'll find her," as if I had a great new plan.

The car got real quiet.

"I promise," I said.

"Yeah," Peep said, soft.

"This building must be temporary," I said. "While they renovate. They're building the real museum around back, or down the road, or something."

"The Hall of Fame doesn't matter," she said, huddling by her door. "Momma's the only thing."

She was right. Getting us here was nothing, not without Momma.

"Where are we going to sleep?" she asked.

Sleeping had not been part of my plan. We were supposed to make it to Flench, pick up Momma, and be back by bedtime. We should have been tucked into our own beds by now, warm as toast. Or me and Momma headed off on our chicken tour . . .

"We can sleep here." I patted the seat next to me and smiled. "It'll be like camping," I said in my best fake-happy voice. Like when Daddy rang up a sale for one discounted Econo-tread. He thanked the customer like he was busting with joy. Less than a dollar's commission, and his feet hurt and he had one of his headaches, but the man who bought that tire never knew. It was back home when the truth came out, part of it anyway. He left work laughing with Ed and Miss Jeannie, ho, ho, ho, but Daddy wouldn't let us forget how hard he worked.

I glanced at Peep and added a little chuckle, like this would be F-U-N, but she wasn't buying it. "I can't sleep here," Peep said, stern, like sleeping in a car was against her religion.

"We'll be ready to romp, bright and early," I said. "If we sleep here, we won't miss a thing."

"We won't miss Momma, you mean," Peep said.

I swallowed hard, missing Momma, missing her so

bad I couldn't breathe. "Nope," I said. Inhale. Smile. Exhale. "We won't."

Peep unwound the seat belt from her hand. Red welts ringed her arm like angry bracelets. "Okay," she said. "I get the backseat." She climbed over the seat, without a fight, or a kick, or another nasty word, and settled down real gentle.

"Say your prayers before we go to sleep," I said, like everything was regular. Me, the big girl, tucking her in for the night. Peep would say them for us both. The sister who skips homework and steals cars shouldn't be the family representative to God.

Peep mumbled something about manna (which made my stomach growl real bad) and dying before you wake (which didn't put me in a mood to close my eyes).

Still I tried.

I pulled Daddy's jacket tighter and tried to think of warm things. Hot chocolate with marshmallows melted on top, so hot they scorched my tongue. Walking barefoot on the road in August, till the soles of my feet blistered. Pulling toast out of the toaster. "Don't burn your fingers!" Momma would yell across the kitchen, like I'd hurt myself if she didn't warn me off.

If I didn't find Momma, who'd warn me?

Outside, a few stars struggled to shine through the clouds, the same stars that were over Momma's head. She was probably looking out her window, just like me, right this minute. She was probably seeing Venus and that round-faced Man in the Moon. She could pick the brightest star, just beneath that big dark cloud, and whisper a silent wish.

I would make that wish, too.

If I should die before I wake . . .

I traced those ballpoint lines on my palm. How far had I really traveled? Had I made any progress at all?

"What do you think Daddy's doing?" Peep asked.

Right away every one of my muscles tensed.

Daddy was in his brass bed, wrapped up in the green feather quilt, snoring. Dreaming of tires and glory.

It went quiet again, quiet enough for thoughts to build like storm clouds inside my head. Memories of Daddy and me. Stuff I didn't let myself think of back home.

Inhale. Smile. Exhale.

When I was in kindergarten.

Breathe.

Mrs. Crouch threw her hands up in the air, all dramatic, and said we'd create something special for Father's Day.

I loved Mrs. Crouch and I loved Father's Day, and I wanted to create so bad my stomach cramped.

All us kids stood by our tables while she passed plastic coffee can lids down the row. "No pushing," she said, while she poured plaster of paris into each one, plaster thick and so white it was nearly blue.

"Press your palms into the plaster," she told us, after a minute or two.

Lasting impressions of our own little hands.

"Now hold still," she warned.

I was still. Still. STILL so my little print would last forever.

But I was a full head taller than the others, and my hands were paws, with raggedy hangnails, and blunt fingertips, and I couldn't stop chewing below the quick, even when the skin stung and bled. Even when Daddy yelled, "Get your hand out of your mouth." Even when Momma painted my fingertips with peppery oil.

I stomped my fat palm into that wet plaster, ice cold at first, then warm, then nearly hot. I held STILL. And when I pulled my hand away, my mark was ugly.

Daddy's lasting impression of me.

"Line up, children," Mrs. Crouch said. So the good ones walked quick and polite, all in a row, down to the restroom, to wash away the sticky plaster.

I moved slow.

My class filed out the door as I slipped to Kathy Nelson's spot, second table from the left. I fingered the quivering whiteness suspended in her lid, her teensy handprint trapped there, forever.

In one quick swipe, I snatched it. Swapped our lids. My ugly mark for her delicate fingers, her miniature palm for my blob. I stuck my pencil into Kathy's hardening plaster and scratched "To Daddy, Love Margie," and I put it in the middle of my table.

Now it was mine.

I ran to the end of the bathroom line and waited my turn, leaning against the concrete block wall, like I was bored and everything took too long.

Back in the classroom, Kathy poked the switcheroo and shoved it to the edge of the table. "Maybe plaster goes lumpy when it dries," she said, like that made any sense. I kept quiet, counting the holes in every ceiling tile.

The bell rang and I marched home, careful with my plaster round, smooth and white as a hen's egg. Kathy's handprint and my name, wrapped up safe, in pink tissue paper.

I gave it to Daddy, on Father's Day Sunday morning, nestled up against his apple-cinnamon pancakes. He smiled real big, unwrapping the tissue. He tweaked my nose, like he loved me.

Eye winker.

Tom tinker.

Nose dropper.

Chin chopper.

Daddy tickled me, gentle, under my chin and he hung that plaque on the wall behind his chair. "I'm proud of you," he said to me, me, me.

No.

Not me.

The rain started up again, drip,

                        drip,

                                drip—

then a flood. Water filmed the windows, turning them into silvery mirrors. I sat up, clutching the Faithful Ford's shiny key in my thick, rough hand, squinting to see.

But there was no reflection.

Nothing.

Not one trace of me.

22

Hours passed, the clouds moved on, and the whole stupid world woke up. Dogs whined by back doors, waiting to be let out. Kids crawled out of their beds, pulling on yesterday's blue jeans. And I opened my eyes, peeling my face from the Arctic Velvette.

Some places look nicer in daylight, sun streaming the shadows away. Daytime windows sparkle. Shiny doors invite you inside. But the Hall of Fame was not one of those places. In the light of day it was even more of a dump. The shutters sagged, and the front porch looked like it was held on with one rusty nail, more chicken coop than chicken museum.

In the backseat, Peep snuffled, loud and piggy. Drool dribbled from the corner of her mouth and her hair stood up in a tangled web. Nobody would call her Pretty Little Princess anymore.

"Rise and shine," I said, loud and cheerful, because I was the grownup. Because I could fake-smile. Because I knew how to lie.

"The square root of 463 is *xyz*," she mumbled, but didn't open her eyes. She had to be the only person in the universe who solved math problems in her sleep. Otherwise all of humanity was in big trouble. A planet can only hold so many evil geniuses.

Momma would be up and dressed by now, neat starched blouse and a little blue sweater draped cozy across her shoulders. One last flip through her "Pocket Guide to Poultry Collectibles." Check. A final tick down her list: Henny Penny Coin Canister, Mint New in Box.

Ready to romp.

Back home, Daddy was waking up, too. He would swing his long skinny legs out from underneath the covers, and poke his feet at the rug, to find his house shoes. He would stumble to flick on the light switch, calling down the hall for me and Peep to get up. Then he'd remember: We weren't there. Momma was gone, too.

Was he sad?

Or relieved?

I leaned over the seat and joggled Peep's shoulder, and finally she opened one eye.

"It's morning," I said. "Let's go."

"I'm starving," she answered, yawning.

"We don't have money for breakfast," I said, like I didn't remember there would have been plenty if she hadn't spent her dimes on candy. If she hadn't gobbled it all up, greedy, by herself. But I wouldn't rise to her bait. I would pretend I wasn't hungry. Grownups ignored their growling stomachs when they had a job to do.

"I bet Daddy's having eggs for breakfast," Peep said, rubbing it in.

Yes. Daddy was eating eggs. Sunny-side up. He'd slash them with his fork and mop the yolks with a biscuit. He'd wolf every scrap. "I couldn't care less what he's eating," I said. That got her. Victory to Margie.

She closed her big mouth long enough to climb out of the car, eyes blinking in the sunshine, lashes fluttering, like a movie star posing for a close-up.

"Momma's probably at her hotel, pressing wrinkles from her skirt or—" I said, before she had a chance to ask. But she didn't care what I thought, smacking past me up the Hall of Fame's steps, yanking the rickety door open and slamming it in my face.

"I'm not sure they're open yet," I called, but Peep had disappeared inside.

The Hall of Fame was dark. And it stunk, oldy moldy. But not can't-afford-the-light-bill dark, or damp-around-the-corners mold. This was precious antique mold. Museums kept the lights off on purpose, to preserve their precious exhibits. Right? And there must be antique chickens in here. Valuable and sure to stink, no matter how hard you scrubbed them.

Finally my eyes adjusted to the shadows. From the rooster red carpet to the eggshell ceiling, the whole place was stuffed with fine-feathered friends. Taxidermied chickens with real feathers huddled just beneath the ceiling, glass and china hens strutted around the walls.

But where were the Rooster Rompers? Where were the crowds? We were too early. The place wasn't open yet and—

I'd barely made it across the little chick welcome mat when a rack of duck decoys rustled and an old woman, more ancient than any museum exhibit, stepped out of the shadows. Her dress was gray and droopy and her long skinny shoes looked like something pulled off a trick-or-treat witch. "Can I help you?" she creaked.

"I'm sorry, but my sister ran in here and I know you're not open yet and—" I held my hand tight against my leg so she wouldn't see the ink smears sketched across my palm and think I was some little baby who couldn't be left alone with a ballpoint pen without writing all over herself.

"We're looking for our Momma," Peep said, appearing suddenly, right at my elbow.

"We're open, but ain't nobody here but us chickens," the woman cackled. "You can call me Aunt Blanche."

I didn't know why we needed to call her anything— much less Aunt. As soon as Momma walked through the door we'd grab up what she needed and we'd hop in the Faithful Ford and that would be the end of all this. Fresh start. New beginning. No—what did she say her name was?—Aunt Blanche hanging around our necks. We'd be out of here.

Peep couldn't resist politeness, even if it didn't make sense. "My name's Peep," she said, sugar sweet. "This is Margie."

"Glad to meet you girls. Make yourself at home," Aunt Blanche said.

Fine. She was being nice, not saying "Hands to yourself" and "No children allowed without a parent." But the way she said "home" was like a teeny-tiny knife plunged into my heart. Chickens or no chickens, this place wasn't a home. Home was soup on the stove, and the smell of that rosy air freshener Momma liked, and the perfect edge Daddy made when he cut the grass, and Jimmy popping wheelies on his bike as he sped down Elm Street and . . .

But me and Momma would be driving on, to all those chicken spots. Who knew if we'd ever be home again.

It would be okay, life on the road, long as Momma had her chickens, the whole flock, and I had . . . "Do you have Red Hen Kollectible Keepsakes?" I asked.

"Largest selection in the U.S. of A." Aunt Blanche waved her duster toward a case by the cash register. An altar to the Little Red Hen Collection. Hens, chicks, roosters, all of them were posed inside, almost solemn behind the glass, like animals of the Nativity. Their feathers were glazed bright. Their beaks tilted just so. And Momma's prize was front and center, cradled in her ceramic manger.

The Henny Penny Coin Canister.

Limited Edition.

Eggsclusively at the International Poultry Hall of Fame.

Every one of Henny Penny's brush-stroked feathers was gold-tipped. Her beady eyes glittered like diamonds. Now I understood everything.

Peep could call me whatever she liked, but if Henny Penny was here, Momma would be here, too.

100% Money-Back Guarantee.

"Could you tell us when the tours start?" Peep asked.

"Tours?" Aunt Blanche flicked her duster over a sea-shell barnyard.

"Margie said there were special tours today. For the Rooster Romp, Hens of Distinction, and World's Most Famous Bird."

"I never said . . ." Well, not exactly.

"Oh, the Rooster Romp?" Aunt Blanche said. "Sale table's in the back."

And without so much as a pocketful of jingling dimes to warn me, Peep hauled off and punched me, right in the arm.

"What was that for?" I said.

"See the sign?" she said, pointing to a table in the back of the room. A cardboard rooster cutout had *Rooster Romp 15% Off* lettered across his chest.

"This isn't a museum," Peep said, poking a hen-and-chick saltshaker. "It's a store. A gift shop full of ugly leftovers nobody wants."

It's true there were price tags on most everything. Okay, every exhibit had a price. And they didn't look exactly like museum exhibits, more like store displays, but—

Peep punched me again.

"Who cares if it's a sale or a museum? What difference does it make?" I took a step back, out of range of Peep's swing. "As long as Momma comes . . ."

"Nothing matters to you. Nothing," Peep said. "Not stealing or kidnapping or . . ."

T-totally wrong. Everything mattered to me. Too much.

Aunt Blanche stepped in between us. "You two in some sort of trouble?"

"We're not in trouble," I said. "We're just waiting for our momma."

"You're a big fat liar," Peep said. "We're in big trouble. Margie said Momma would be here, and we slept in the car last night waiting."

"I was just . . ."

Aunt Blanche put down her duster and cleared her throat, like that would shut Peep down.

"And Margie stole Daddy's car, and the police chased us, and . . ."

"The police did not chase us," I said.

"You thought it was the police."

$<<<$ vs. $>>>$

Greater than screaming open-mouthed at *Less than*.

$P > M$

"And Momma's not coming. She never was coming. This whole thing was Margie's crazy imagination," Peep said, face falling, out of steam. Speaking the gospel truth at last.

"I see," said Aunt Blanche.

No. She didn't see anything. She couldn't see my heart. How I tried. How I drove. How I took care. How this was my chance. My only chance.

She couldn't see the map inside of me.

23

My Map of Me had chickens in the center, at the heart. That's where Momma's heart was, with her chickens. All along the edges of the Map were black rings. Tires for Daddy. There were math facts and vocab words sprinkled around, for all the stuff Peep spouted, on and on.

That was the Map of Me. A map that didn't show one bit of me myself. Because there wasn't anything to show.

How could somebody turn in a thing like that? How could I show that to the world?

I breathed in and out and in again. "Momma will be here," I said, like that was the final word. Then I pulled the note from my pocket, turning it over, smoothing it against my palm.

EXHIBITS!

REFRESHMENTS!

RARE POULTRY COLLECTIBLES!

Momma wrote her note on the Rooster Romp advertisement for a reason. She was after that little Henny Penny, and when she had it she'd be complete.

But Smarty-Peep did not understand, or didn't care, or just wanted to keep raising her ruckus. "I want to go home," she said. "I want Daddy."

"No," I said.

Momma had started us out on this trip. Daddy wasn't going to end it.

24

Seen lots of folks bit by chicken fever," Aunt Blanche said. "Your momma desperate to adopt that little chick? That makes perfect sense to me." Aunt Blanche talked like Momma, like that canister was alive, bursting full of poultry magic. Like me and Peep should just accept it.

"It doesn't make sense to me. Momma never should have left." Peep folded her arms across her chest, blubbering. "She's not coming and I want Daddy."

"No," I said for the ten-millionth time. "Not Daddy." Momma shouldn't have gone off. Okay. But Daddy was the last thing I needed. No. The last thing *we* needed, both of us, me and Peep. He'd storm in, flapping and crowing like a rooster in this henhouse of a gift shop. If he bothered to come at all.

And which would be worse?

I shook my head.

Peep didn't get it. This trip hadn't taught her anything. I had to protect her whether she liked it or not.

I trailed my finger across the Country Creatures farm display, past the Pick-Nick-Chicks, nonchalant, like I knew what to do next.

It was what, 9:30? 10:00? Momma hadn't shown up. Not one single customer had shown up, other than me and Peep, and we weren't buying. Aunt Blanche and Peep wandered off, one dusting, the other sulking. And finally I'd poked on just about everything you could print, mold, or carve in the shape of a chicken.

Maybe Peep was right. Momma wasn't coming. Maybe I had to take Henny Penny, the magical chick, to *her*. Maybe bringing that chicken to Momma was what that Hobbit man would have called My Destiny or My Quest or something else goofy-sounding. All I knew was I was meant to have that chicken. And to give it to Momma.

The display case was closed with a tiny key, but, just like the key in the Faithful Ford's ignition, it turned easy. Click. Open sesame. I took the chicken from her manger, cradling her in my palm. So little, she wouldn't hold more than a dozen quarters, or a handful of Peep's precious dimes. But to Momma this chicken was worth her weight in gold and diamonds. She was the key to Momma's heart.

If Momma had this chicken, things would be different.

Her black eyes would sparkle, tracing the hand-painted feathers, holding the precision-molded golden beak to the light.

Henny Penny would bring Momma back. We'd go home complete.

Or . . .

It wouldn't matter. Me and Momma would whiz down the highway: Rhode Island to San Diego and on, forever.

I turned Henny Penny over in my hand, admiring her shiny red comb, those delicate clawed feet, not planning to slip her in my pocket. Not really.

Even though she would nestle so sweet next to the Faithful Ford's key. Even though it was only four steps to the door and fifteen more to the car. Even though no one here would miss me until I was long gone. And Momma's face would light up when I pulled Henny Penny from my pocket and placed her, gentle, in her hands, like I'd given her the sun, moon, and stars. Like I'd given her everything.

I'd pay Aunt Blanche back, sure, soon as . . . soon as . . .

Henny Penny shimmered in my smeary palm. Magic. I was not a thief. I didn't take her. I would have placed her back on that shelf, honest. I was almost ready to slip her back into her niche, careful, delicate, graceful, when—

Aunt Blanche snuck up behind me, like a thief in the night, and slapped that feather duster across my arm.

If I jumped an inch I jumped a yard. And Henny Penny quivered. Aunt Blanche's gnarled fingers curled toward me, groping, and I reached the treasure toward her hand. Careful. I was careful. Very careful.

I did what I was supposed to do, just right.

I placed that chicken right into her outstretched hand.

But her hand didn't grip.

And Henny Penny somersaulted, past that old hag's wrinkled claw, past my thick paw, down, down, down, twirling, like me and Peep in the Faithful Ford.

Spinning.

Like Jimmy on the gym floor.

Twirling.

Like all those tires on the Map of Me.

Down.

Till Henny Penny smacked against the concrete floor.

Beak first.

25

She was smashed, dashed into a million zillion tiny pieces. Red comb, mixed with yellow beak, mixed with black feathers into hand-painted 100 percent porcelain collector's quality gravel, all over the floor.

"You did that on purpose," I shouted.

"Mmm . . . mmm . . . mmm, that blasted chicken slipped right through my fingers," Aunt Blanche said, like breaking Momma's wish upon a star was nothing.

"It's your fault."

She didn't bother to deny it, pulling a little red broom and dustpan from behind the counter.

Cluck Cluck Cluck. Her tongue ticked the roof of her mouth and the broom brushed the concrete floor and the shards dashed the metal dustpan. *Cluck Cluck Cluck.*

My eyes stung. I did not cry. Never. Ever. But pretty

soon my face was dripping wet with tears I'd held inside all day and all night. All week. All year. I'd held those tears, walled them up, my whole life. Now they busted through, and poured out. I didn't care if Aunt Blanche saw. Peep either. She'd appeared, stiff, across from me. I didn't care if she got a big eyeful of me crying. Too bad. "Momma needed that Henny Penny," I sobbed. "I needed it, too."

"Oh, honey," Aunt Blanche said, putting the broom and dustpan down on the floor, trying to take me between her scrawny arms. I wanted to push her away, but there was no more push inside me. She hugged me tight, tight, tight.

And I didn't break.

"That bird wasn't anything but a chunk of old red clay," she whispered, pushing the hair from my eyes with her gnarled hand. "It couldn't bring your momma back. There was no magic there."

No. She was wrong. That chicken meant the world to Momma. All the chickens, they were everything to her.

Aunt Blanche held me like she'd never let me go. And then there were other arms around me, too. Peep's arms. Her sweet cotton-candy breath teased my shoulder and everything was quiet, just Aunt Blanche's *cluck, cluck, cluck* and Peep's soft breath.

Wrapped up in Aunt Blanche's arms, and Peep's, no pinching or accusing, just held tight . . . Was this what safe felt like?

For a second, just one teensy-weensy second, I wondered what it would be like to live with Aunt Blanche. Aunt Blanche for our mother, me and Peep her little chicks.

But wouldn't the hugging be too much? And when she saw the real me, the one on the Map, the one who didn't exist—what then?

26

I plucked at the bits that used to be Henny Penny, wing, claw, shining eye. Scattered shards of pottery, hollow inside. Aunt Blanche knelt beside me. "Honey, this is nothing but a broken pot."

"I wanted to bring Momma back and make everything right." I swallowed twice, then three times. "And I just made it worse."

"Not worse. Most people don't do anything to solve their troubles but sit down and cry."

Peep studied her shoes like they were the world's most interesting patent leathers.

"All I wanted was to do one thing good," I said. "One thing that wasn't a mistake."

Aunt Blanche rubbed my arm. "What are you talking about, baby? There's lots of good things."

Peep stared at those shoes even harder. She knew the truth about me.

"I wanted to be equal," I said.

Aunt Blanche let out a little snort and looked from me to Peep, then back to me. "There ain't no such thing as equal," she said. "Not with people."

"Thomas Jefferson said all men are created equal," Peep said. "That means girls, too." She'd paid attention during History of the American Revolution—Declaration of Independence. Of course.

"You don't measure people one against the other, Thomas Jefferson or George Washington or the man who invented fried chicken. There ain't no scale to weigh souls one against the other." Aunt Blanche lifted Henny Penny's shattered tail from the rubble and held it in front of my face. "You see this chicken? Real valuable. They say it's a limited edition."

"Yes, ma'am. I'm sorry I . . ."

Aunt Blanche leaned so close I could feel her warm breath on my cheek. "Margie, honey, stop your thinking. Just listen," she said, barely louder than a whisper, like she was telling a deep dark secret. "This chicken was made out of clay and poured in a mold. I've got a dozen more just like it back in the storeroom. Every one of them equal."

Fine. So what? I didn't need to know how they made chicken canisters. That was the kind of thing Peep cared about. She'd make a poster about it and bring it up to the front of the class and . . .

"Your momma and daddy," Aunt Blanche said, still quiet but more urgent now. "They ain't got a dozen like you."

They were probably relieved about that.

"Maybe it's time you stopped trying to measure yourself against everybody else."

"But . . ."

Aunt Blanche didn't understand what it was like living with a sister like Peep, living up to the expectations of a super seller like Daddy. She might have sparkly glasses and weird clothes and spout a bunch of weird ideas, but she didn't know anything.

Momma was gone.

I'd never be as good as Peep.

And Daddy didn't care.

"Margie, honey, you made a grand gesture to get your momma back. That's good and brave and true and way more than most would ever dream of."

I swallowed and plucked another shard from the floor. A claw, maybe.

I didn't believe her saying what I'd done was good. Daddy wouldn't believe her either. All the mistakes, all those little debts I'd racked up, he'd add them and multiply them and charge them back to me, with interest.

Peep would probably help him do the math.

27

I'm going to find her," I said. "Wherever she is. And we'll go off and—"

Aunt Blanche cupped my chin in her rough palm and pulled my face up, my blue eyes level with her beady dark ones. "You found your way here, honey. You did real good," she said. "Maybe your momma needs to find her way, too."

"But she needs—"

"You can't grab your momma up and carry her home like some ceramic chick."

"I didn't say she had to change. I'm okay with her collecting. We aren't even going home. We're going—"

Peep shifted like a scared foal and Aunt Blanche's eyes flickered, magnified in those glasses, forcing me to stop. Forcing me to really, truly think.

One thought.

One memory.

Last week.

The way it really happened, not just the way I wanted to tell it.

I woke up in the middle of the night and I wandered into the kitchen to get a drink of water. The back door was standing open, like we lived in a barn. Wind sounds whipped through the trees, over the frost-covered grass, right through the door and across the linoleum. I walked to the door to close it and I saw someone outside. Lying down in the yard.

"Momma?" I said.

Hush . . . called the wind.

I tiptoed out.

She was flat against the grass, face up to the stars, smiling, but barely blinking. She didn't say a word. Her breath made no sound.

"What are you doing out here?" I asked.

"Watching." Her lips didn't seem to move.

Watching the stars probably. Dancing across the sky, trading places, ascending and descending. Orbiting and twirling. Stars and planets and suns and moons. Minuet and tango and waltz in and out of their planetary houses. Gypsy kind of stuff. We did not cover those subjects at Jesse Stuart Elementary.

I dropped to the ground beside Momma. Frosty dew

went right through my pajama pants. My face was wet, too. Tears?

Momma's back was pressed deep into the grass. She must have been soaked. Her hand was ice cold.

"Waiting," she said.

For what? For summer and no school, lemonade and ballgames?

No. I knew it was none of those things.

"For chickens?" I asked.

Momma's laughter jingled, light across the yard, up the trees, into the open air. Not chickens? Then what else? Her eyes were still on the sky, but she didn't seem to see those stars anymore.

"Good night, Momma," I said, and I crept back to my room.

Those witchy clothes, this weird place, Aunt Blanche knew. She saw inside me like she was magic. And she was right.

Leaving was not about me or chickens.

It was Momma.

Inside her heart.

She had to draw her own map, across the stars, to someplace none of the rest of us could go.

28

I think we need to call Daddy," I said, taking Peep's hand in mine.

Aunt Blanche led me around the counter and I followed, right hand shoved in my pocket, clenching my fist around the Faithful Ford's key so tight its teeth bit into my palm. I'd call Daddy, and I'd take the consequences, and if he didn't answer, fine. Okay, fine.

Aunt Blanche pointed to an old black phone. I held the heavy receiver to my ear and punched in the numbers. Even the ring sounded old and buzzy, like wires stretched too far, almost to snapping, too many miles back to our house, too far for Momma. I understood that now. But was it too far for me?

One . . . three . . . five rings. No answer. Good. I didn't have to talk. I'd leave a message. I'd slip outside. I'd go off to the next chicken place on my own. Aunt Blanche would see to Peep and . . .

As I lowered the phone to the cradle I caught a click, then a voice, calling, shouting through the wires. "Hello? World of . . . I mean, this is Perry Tempest."

I whipped the phone back to my ear.

"Hello?" Daddy said again, but he didn't sound right. His voice was gravelly and squeaky at the same time, like maybe he was sick or maybe . . . "Is anybody there? Hello?"

I sucked in a breath. "Daddy? It's me," I said, but barely a sound came out.

"Marjorie Ann? Where are you?" This time he barked the words, fast and sharp.

"We're in Flench, at the International Poultry Hall of Fame." My voice wasn't my own. Too trembly. Too slow. Too unsure of the next word. "Daddy? Come get us," I said, but the line had already buzzed dead.

"Is he coming?" Peep asked.

And for once I didn't try to protect her or hide the truth. I didn't try to make up stories, not even to myself. I laid it out straight. "I don't know."

29

Aunt Blanche fluttered, like she had all kinds of work to do counting her eggs, hatched and unhatched. But as me and Peep sat on a bench by the door, waiting and waiting and waiting, Aunt Blanche's fluttering turned to hovering, and finally she was right up on top of us. "Quick as your daddy comes I'll run and get you girls some lunch" and "You sure that jacket's warm enough for you, honey? It looks a mite thin and you really ought to—"

"I'm plenty warm," I said.

"Tomorrow's Saturday," she said. "That's market day in Flench, and if you two are still here—I mean, if your daddy can bring you back over, I could show you . . ."

Peep tilted her chin up toward the old woman, focusing those sad blue eyes on her. "Do you have any children, Aunt Blanche?"

She took a step back and snorted. "Children?" She waved her feather duster in the air. "What would I be needing children for, when I've got all this?" she said, practiced, like she'd said the same thing a million times before.

"You're right," I said. What did Aunt Blanche need with a couple of kids? What did anybody need with . . .

Then before I had the chance to think about what we'd do if Daddy didn't come, and what we'd do if he did, I saw a flash through the window. A pair of shiny black wingtips, long and heavy, connected to a pair of legs, gray flannel, clip-clopping up the sidewalk.

Daddy had come.

Run! Run! Run away! my feet said. *This is your last chance. Take that key. Get out of here.* But my heart glued me to the bench.

Daddy nearly walked past the Faithful Ford, then— he stopped, running his hand along its silky fender. No smashes. No bashes. I'd taken care of his baby. I hadn't hurt it. I hadn't hurt anything, not too bad. Not permanent.

Peep saw Daddy, too, but she didn't move, or didn't seem to, because everything was moving slow, like we were wading through deep water. Daddy climbed the steps, one, then two, squaring his shoulders, taking a breath. Then the door swung open, and he was there.

Not crisp and starched. Rumpled. My eyes could hardly focus on the wrinkles across his shirt. And his tie. No tie.

Daddy out of the house on Friday morning with no tie.

His eyes darted from the Chipper Chicks to the Rooster Romp table, squinting in the dim light. But before he could see straight, Peep leaped from her chair and plastered herself against his chest.

This time my heart said *Jump! Follow her!* But that slippery thing inside me, wherever fear sprang from, held me down.

"Baby!" he said to Peep, all surprised to see his precious girl.

I breathed. He would not "baby" me. He couldn't even see me, hidden in the shadows.

His eyes moved back and forth, around the room, rooster to hen. And when he found Aunt Blanche, back there with her broom, a flush ran up his neck and across his cheeks, tempera red against his school-paste skin. His Adam's apple bobbed twice, fast, almost too fast to see, then his lips peeled into his wolf smile. "How do!" he called out, like he was selling Aunt Blanche a set of tires. "I'm sorry my girls have put you to so much trouble."

Aunt Blanche's penciled-on eyebrows popped up, but *switch switch switch* she and her broom focused on the dust under the bristles like she was panning for gold. And *cluck, cluck, cluck* she held her tongue.

"You know how kids are." Daddy's voice boomed, too loud for the little room, rattling Aunt Blanche's chickens on their racks, just like he did at home.

"Yes, I do," Aunt Blanche said, pronouncing each syllable sharp.

Peep looked over her shoulder, urging me, but no way I was joining their little clump. I didn't belong. I knew the truth.

I'd speak the truth, too.

"I stole your car."

Daddy's chin snapped up, and he looked me in the eye, surprised to see me—like, did he hope I wasn't here? But his smile held, stuck up in both corners, dimples practically starched. "That's nothing," he said.

I took his car. I kidnapped Peep. I did my best to bring Momma home.

Nothing?

I faded deeper into the shadows.

144

"You look tired, Daddy," Peep said, hugging him around the belly, both of them grinning like fools, like they both thought I was a great big nothing.

"I *am* tired, baby. I've been driving all night, looking for you."

"Is Momma home?" Peep asked, still believing in Sleeping Beauty endings. This trip hadn't opened her eyes, not one bit.

Daddy's Adam's apple bobbed up and down and up. He glanced fast at Aunt Blanche, then down at his shoes. "Your momma . . . She went . . . I'll . . ." he said, like words were glued inside his mouth. His chin dipped to his chest and he seemed to shrink right before my eyes, deflating like an old birthday balloon, from hero-size, to normal, to smaller.

"We aren't the boss of her," I said. "Momma has her own map, one inside her. In her heart."

Daddy's head jerked up like I'd slapped him.

"She'll come back when she finds her own way," I said.

Aunt Blanche cleared her throat real loud and gave her head a little shake. Maybe now wasn't the time for me to spout everything I'd learned.

But Daddy met me, eye to eye, understanding, knowing, accepting.

His wolf smile had melted into two straight lines, one lip over the other.

=

Sad and scared and lonely.

Equal.

All three of us.

Plus one for Momma.

Sad + Scared + Lonely + Lost.

We were all the same.

30

Aunt Blanche waved us off, pressing fluffy cotton-ball chicks into me and Peep's hands, even though Easter was two months away.

"You two come back," she said.

"We three," Peep said.

Maybe.

We walked out the door, all three of us, Daddy holding Peep's hand, Peep holding mine.

Quick as we left those rickety porch steps Peep gave a little skip. Fooling around. Silly. "Don't step on the crack, Margie!" she said, and Daddy laughed one of his billy goat chuckles.

I picked my feet up and placed them down precise.

No bad luck for me.

Until Peep brought it on.

Her feet stopped moving right in the middle of the sidewalk. "Margie can't go home," she said, like her brain had been hit by some memory tidal wave and all of a sudden had total recall. "She broke Jimmy McDonald's ankle and everybody at Jesse Stuart hates her."

I went stiff and yanked my hand away.

"Shoot!" Daddy said, which was close as he'd ever come to cussing. "I saw Jimmy out on the road this morning, racing that rusty bicycle of his. He's just fine."

Just fine. Peep had said I maimed him for life. Destroyed him. Who was the liar-liar-pants-on-fire now? But still Daddy didn't reach out to grab my hand.

Ed had given Daddy a ride to Flench and then gone on back, so we Tempests climbed into the Faithful Ford, all together by ourselves. A family almost. Daddy leaned his left elbow against the driver's side window, natural, steering with one hand. Cool. Experienced. The way I wanted to look behind the wheel. I sat still. Peep, being halfway a big old baby, she fell asleep in the backseat, right off.

Then it was left to just Daddy and me. And it was quiet, real quiet, nothing to say. Miles rolled past, and I remembered to breathe, about two thousand times, and I finally said, "It's not nothing."

Daddy jumped at the sound of my voice like I'd

slipped five pounds of red-hot potatoes underneath him. "What?" he said.

"It's not nothing," I repeated. "Me taking your car and driving here."

One potato, two potato, seconds ticked past. Daddy shifted in his seat. I took a breath. I made myself remember how his lips made those lines. Equals. Equals. Equals. I could say these things.

"I wanted to bring Momma home," I said. "That's why I took your car."

"You won't do that again," he said, soft, like what I'd do was a known fact.

"No, sir. I won't."

He put his left hand on the steering wheel, setting his right hand free, smooth, a real driver. Then he reached that right hand across that wide Arctic Velvette gulf, that icy blue channel, and settled his strong hand, his long tapered fingers, over mine.

"That was a crazy stunt, Marjorie Ann," he said. "But going to look for your momma, that was brave." Daddy's Adam's apple bobbed and his equals sign crumpled.

"She'll be back," I said.

"I know." Quiet as a whisper. Then he patted my hand, tender as a hug, and my hand, my big old hand, with chewed-up nails and ink-pen tattoos, it felt beautiful. Prettier than that little plaster print. All me.

I turned my hand over, palm up. Those ballpoint streaks were half faded, smeared into my palm's creases, marking out the real Margie, like some Gypsy palm reader's chart.

Health line.

Heart line.

Life line.

The real, true Map of Me.

Written across my own hand, big and strong.

Daddy proud of me.

Me proud of myself.

"I love you, Daddy," I said.

He smiled big and bright, not a wolf smile, not a "Have I got a deal for you" smile. A real smile. And I smiled, too.

"Can I have my key now?" he asked.

I dropped the shiny silver key into his palm and he took my hand back in his, my Map of Me nestled into his strong, steady grip.

And we wound our way back home.

Acknowledgments

Sometimes a road runs straight, but other times, as with this novel, the trip is long and winding. Many people led me, directing me along this story's true course. The Society of Children's Book Writers and Illustrators' Work-in-Progress Grant gave me early encouragement, acknowledging that I was on the right path. Thank you to my writing friends, Zu, Rose, Debbie, Barb, Vicki, Nicole, Catherine, and Sarah, for keeping me on track and urging me onward. My Vermont College advisers, Norma Fox Mazer, Jane Resh Thomas, Tim Wynne-Jones, Kathi Appelt, and Carolyn Coman, held the compass, challenging me to explore dark and dangerous territory. As I drew closer, my agent Sarah Davies found the perfect home for Margie, Peep, and me and helped all three of us settle in. My wonderful editors, Melanie Kroupa and Beth Potter, always seemed to know the way. Finally, thanks to my family, David, Julia, and Will, for sending me off on this journey and welcoming me back.